D1519218

ISBN: 9798398953787

# CHAPTER ONE

*Clifton, Virginia*
*The 1990s*

CHILDREN WERE EASY TARGETS. Naturally. So the man considered himself fortunate that the beginning stage of his undertaking involved a child. Had the parameters been different, he might have been forced to engage a full-grown adult, possibly armed.

Fate had been kind, however.

His first kill was going to be a little girl.

He crouched in the darkness of the forest, watching the trio of children through the trees. The girls' faces strobed orange and yellow with the campfire's light in front of them. A scent of burning wood lingered in the air; the man smelled it, tasted it.

He assessed the girls—their faces on the brink of impending maturity; long beanpole legs; chipped nail polish from homemade manicures—and placed all three around the age of twelve. They wore T-shirts bearing images of country music sensation Chelsi Nichols—that wild-red-haired beauty with vivacious energy and a 100-watt smile to match. The children had brought a portable stereo with them, and they were playing Nichols's most famous song, keeping the volume low—just a gentle background ambiance to their conversation. The muted notes carried off the tree trunks.

The man watched silently as the girls giggled and guffawed and whispered and shouted around the fire. They were rooted to their upturned logs and had been like this for half an hour. Patience was key; eventually, the group would have to disperse. After all, the concert was to begin in less than three hours, and the venue was thirty miles away. If fate continued to shine favorably on the man, when the girls finally left, they would head in different directions.

The man needed one of them alone.

Just one.

He continued to watch.

———

Seated at the fire with two popular girls, Heather fought to maintain her composure. The forced smile was making her cheeks ache.

Heather had never been alone amongst the other girls' clique—not outside of school, anyway. Despite her efforts to feign sophistication, her bouncing knee and a nagging sense of not belonging threatened to give her away.

The other two girls—Regina and Jessica—were grinning. Their affability hinted not at innocent exuberance, though, but at impending mischief. Like Heather, they wore Chelsi Nichols T-shirts featuring the singer's broad smile and trademark red curls, which were augmented by loud graphics and garish fonts. Regina and Jessica's shirts were brand-new; Heather's was old. Like, *really* old. At least seven months' worth of heavy use—wearing it to school, washing it, sleeping in it, washing it, wearing it to her grandmother's in Maryland on the weekends, washing it. The shirt was well-faded but well-loved.

Next to Jessica's feet was a small radio with a CD player. Of course, all three girls had brought a copy of Chelsi's latest album to the campfire, but it was Regina's CD playing through the tinny speakers. For the last ten minutes, the trio had been looping Chelsi's mega-hit, "Cabin Nights, City Lights." Once more, Chelsi's voice belted out the chorus.

*The young, the old*, Chelsi sang in butter-smooth tones. *The broken and the bold.*

The three girls were sixth-graders. In Caldera Heights School District, sixth grade was still elementary level, not middle school. Heather had felt childish and restrained all school year, knowing that only ten miles away, Wynona Middle School encompassed grades 6 through 8. If it weren't for a cruel twist of fate and a few imaginary lines on a map, Heather would be a *middle schooler*.

As it was, she was still an elementary school student. A kid.

Now, at the campfire, however, Heather was beginning to appreciate her mandated naiveté because Jessica's continued pressure to drink alcohol was making Heather feel more than uncomfortable...

...she felt panicked, like she should bolt off, just go running away into the trees.

Jessica was thirteen, the oldest of the trio at the campfire. The girl hadn't been held back a year; rather, Jessica's birth month put her among the oldest in sixth grade. Heather was twelve, as was Regina, less than a year younger than Jessica, but Jessica had always used her slight age advantage to augment her already considerable popularity.

In a few hours, Jessica and Regina would go to the concert with some older kids; Heather was going with her mother.

Jessica had called the campfire meeting to "pre-game." Heather hadn't known what that meant, but it hadn't taken her long to figure it out.

Jessica held up the styrofoam cup again, reaching it in Heather's direction. She grinned and gave the cup an inviting shake. The crushed ice and liquid sloshed inside.

"Come *on*, Heather," Jessica said. "I only put, like, that much in." With her free hand, Jessica extended a pair of fingers a half-inch apart. "If I took any more, my old man woulda noticed. He watches his bottles like a hound."

Regina snickered. "No, he watches them like a drunken middle-aged accountant."

Jessica whipped around on her friend. "Shut up, bitch."

Though it was a harsh command, Jessica smiled when she said it, and both of the cool girls laughed. Heather laughed too, trying to maintain as much dignity and credibility as she could, but the laugh was forced, as the word *bitch* had cut right through her. Heather's parents seldom cursed, and Heather never did. As Heather saw it, there would be plenty of time for cursing later in life as an adult.

She stole another glance at those dark trees, again feeling the desire to leave. She didn't belong here, no matter how much she'd tried to convince herself that she did.

Jessica thrust the styrofoam cup once more in Heather's direction.

"It's vodka. No one can smell it on your breath. That's why I chose it. Your mom could be a foot away from you, and she'll never know."

Heather shook her head. "That's okay. Thanks."

Jessica snickered. Not only was she a bit older than the other girls, but she was a bit taller too, a bit larger—just a tad more developed, nearer adolescence, more adult-like. Dark brown hair, silky and straight and parted. Blue eyes that were both beautiful and cold.

Jessica stared into Heather for a moment and flicked her gaze in Regina's direction before turning back to Heather and leaning closer.

"You ever heard of the Bunny Man?" Jessica said, a devilish grin on her face.

Heather nodded. "Of course."

She knew the name and all the gruesome rumors. But Mom had told Heather to disregard the legend, that it would only give her nightmares.

Taking her friend's lead, Regina inched nearer to Heather as well. When she spoke, she lowered her voice for dramatic effect. "Oh, you're in for a treat, Heather."

Regina—a petite girl with shoulder-length, light brown hair—then gave Heather a smile that was as nasty as Jessica's.

Heather didn't respond. She looked back and forth between the other two.

Jessica took a long drag from the styrofoam cup's straw—which screeched against the plastic topper—keeping her blue eyes locked on Heather while she sucked.

Finally, she lowered the cup and said, "It started in 1904. The townspeople of Clifton didn't like having a mental hospital nearby. Can you blame them? But when the patients were being moved to a prison, the bus crashed, and all the crazies escaped. Authorities tracked all of them down—except one."

Heather blinked.

Regina nodded, inching ever closer, coming to the edge of her log.

"He survived in the woods," Regina said with a subtle gesture toward their surroundings. "Weeks passed by, then dead rabbits showed up, hanging from the trees. The man had eaten their flesh, and he wore their hides."

Heather ran her hands together. Of course, she didn't believe what the other two were saying; Heather wasn't a little baby girl. But she was getting worked up all the same. Maybe it was the cool girls' overtly malicious intentions making her heart beat faster, making her palms sweat.

Jessica took over again. "Some school kids found the guy in the woods. And the Bunny Man killed them; he mutilated them like he did the rabbits. He left their corpses hanging near the train bridge over Colchester Road. That's, like, two miles from here."

Jessica paused to dramatically stare into the forest surrounding them. She brought her arms in around herself and shuddered.

Regina laughed.

"In the '70s," Jessica said, "some guy in a bunny suit attacked a man and his girlfriend, chucked a hatchet through their windshield. A week later, someone reported seeing a guy in a bunny suit using a hatchet to chop away at a house under construction. This is real stuff, Heather. My dad kept the newspaper clippings from both of those '70s events. He showed them to me!"

Regina snorted. "Yeah, your dad the drunk."

"Shut up," Jessica said to Regina without taking her eyes off Heather. She brought her elbows to her knees, getting closer, close enough that Heather could see the flames sparkling in her bright blue eyes.

"They say he's still in the trees," Jessica said, whispering now. "Maybe supernatural, maybe not. And that's why people go to the bridge on—"

Heather cut in, taking over to reassert her power in the situation. "On Halloween night. To see if they can find him."

Jessica nodded. "That's right. And the truly brave say his name three times. *Bunny Man. Bunny Man. Bunny Man.* But then it's too late. *Wham!*" She swung her arm. "He'll slice your throat, leave your corpse dangling from the bridge!"

Jessica and Regina laughed.

Heather cautiously scanned the murky depths of the surrounding woods. The Bunny Man was a legend, a childish myth. But Heather couldn't deny the prickling sensation on the back of her neck.

When she returned her attention to Jessica, the slightly older girl extended the cup in Heather's direction again.

"Come on, Heather," Jessica said. "This is your last chance."

Heather shook her head. "No. I don't want to do that."

Both Jessica and Regina laughed mockingly.

"Suit yourself," Jessica said. "Get out of here, then!"

For a moment, Heather couldn't respond. "But ... but your friends were supposed to take me back to my house."

"Should have thought of that a moment ago," Jessica sneered and pointed to the woods. "It's a mile to your house. You got here through those trees."

"There was still daylight then!"

Heather's heart pounded.

"Figure it out," Jessica said with a shrug as she took a long drink through the straw. Then she scowled at Heather and screamed, "*Get the hell out of here!*"

Heather froze in place. Anger and hurt surged through her, and though she detested that it was happening, her eyes moistened. In that paralyzed moment, the other girls stared back at her, their faces smeared with malicious delight, their smiles twisting with cruelty.

Then, fueled by an intense surge of determination, Heather hopped off her log and tore through the tangled undergrowth, tears blurring her vision. Sticks and leaves crunched under her shoes. She stumbled. The space in from of her grew darker rapidly, the scant light from the fire quickly dissipating.

She heard Jessica and Regina cackling after her as she stomped away.

*Go find your mommy, Heather!*

*Change that dingy old shirt when you get home, loser!*

The trees grew darker until the firelight was gone and the only illumination was the faint glow of stars hidden in the cloudy sky above. Heather kept going faster and faster until the jeers faded entirely; all that remained was the silent night air and the whisper of a breeze in the trees.

Her heart pounded in her chest as she fled through the dense undergrowth. Tears streamed down her face. The haunting laughter of the other girls echoed in her ears, but their taunts fueled her determination to get home.

She thought of Mom, less than a mile ahead, through the darkness of the trees. Just a few minutes away. After making it home, a few hours later, Heather and Mom would be in Arlington at the Chelsi Nichols concert. Being there with Mom would be so much better than going with Jessica and Regina and their older friends with their brand-new shirts and their alcohol and their swear words.

But then, a new thought intruded.

One unrelated to Mom and the Chelsi Nichols concert.

The Bunny Man...

With every step she took, Heather's mind raced. The legends of the woods whispered sinister tales of a lurking man and hidden horrors. Although Heather had dismissed the earlier discussion as mere campfire tales, the weight of the actual, verifiable events—the documented cases from the 1970s that Jessica had mentioned—bore down upon Heather now, casting shadows that seemed to move in the corner of her eye.

A sudden sensation of being watched brought her to a halt, her breath catching in her throat. She turned, scanned the trees.

The forest stood silent.

She strained her senses, searching for any sign. Determined to shake off her growing unease, she trudged on. She scolded herself inwardly, reminding herself not to be childish, that the Bunny Man stories were nothing but urban legends.

Yet, the oppressive feeling of being hunted refused to relent. The forest seemed to come alive around her—twigs snapped, leaves rustled, and an eerie breeze hissed through the branches. Her imagination conjured twisted images of the legendary specter, his eyes gleaming with malevolence, his calloused hands reaching out to snatch her away.

She heard something—a distinct noise, like the raspy exhale of a lurking predator. Her heart thundered. She didn't bring herself to a halt again—she *couldn't*—but her head turned instinctively. In the dim light filtering through the trees, she caught a fleeting glimpse of something.

*A person.*

In a fraction of a second, she took in the scant but terrifying details of the silhouette. It was clearly a man. A little under six feet tall. Medium-length hair. He was angled in her direction. And moving.

There was an object in one of his hands.

A hatchet...

The Bunny Man!

Her heart raced, and her stomach clenched as an instinctive wave of terror swept through her.

Without thinking, Heather broke into a desperate run. Tears blurred her vision. Her legs burned as she half-blindly navigated the uneven earth. The sound of approaching footsteps echoed behind her, growing louder, more urgent.

Then, light ahead.

A faint glow far in the distance.

Though she couldn't see any details through the shadowy confusion of the forest, a sense of navigation forged via hours of play in the trees told her exactly what the glow was: the floodlight on the back porch of her house, a security measure her father had installed the previous summer.

She moved faster toward the distant glimmer. Adrenaline fueled her, granting her fleeting bursts of strength. But she couldn't move too quickly—despite her muscle memory sense of geolocation—because twice now, she'd nearly plastered herself into a tree in the darkness.

Plus, the footsteps were closer. If she fell now, the Bunny Man would have her. He was only yards behind her. The footsteps had closed in on her, a predator shrinking the gap.

She stole a glance over her shoulder.

And gasped.

There he was. Right behind her. Running toward her. A shadow among the shadows.

With a surge of adrenaline, she veered to the side, pulling down a slope that she knew would lead her to the faint light ahead, to her house, to Mom and Dad. Her muscles burned in protest as she lunged forward with a desperate surge of strength.

She twisted and dodged. Around the oak tree with the mangled top. Past the boulder she climbed from time to time, the moss-covered one that she'd jokingly named "Mount Heather." To the slope. Now, she would have to—

She slipped.

And fell.

Her butt landed in the leaves, and she skidded down the slope, tumbling forward a few feet before coming to a crunching stop on her knees. She yelped and scrambled to her feet, looked back.

The figure was there.

At the top of the slope.

She still had a lead on him.

She bolted off again.

Faster.

Faster.

Feet pounding the forest floor. Sticks crunching. Hands burning as she used them to push herself past tree trunks, propelling herself forward.

The man gave chase, his heavy footfalls a relentless cadence, drawing ever closer. The distance between them dwindled, his malevolent presence growing more palpable. Panic fueled Heather, her mind locked on the single beacon of safety—the sanctuary of her house.

Just as she thought her lungs would burst, Heather caught another glimpse of the familiar porch light through the trees. It was closer now—close enough she could just make out the house's shape.

Hope surged within her. She pushed herself harder. She could almost feel the warm embrace of home.

But her relief was short-lived.

A figure materialized from the shadows, blocking her path.

The man had passed her by, overtaken her, and closed off her path of escape...

Her mind raced, searching for an explanation, a rationalization for this unforeseen twist, and she quickly remembered the legends once more. Yes, the Bunny Man would know these trees far better than Heather. He'd lived amongst them for decades. Unlike Heather, he could blindly navigate the forest.

Heather came to a sudden stop, her feet scraping in the undergrowth. Her scream tore through the air and echoed off the tree trunks. Somewhere in the forest, a startled animal bolted, its footsteps crunching through the leaves before fading away.

After the scream, Heather's mouth remained open, but the only sound that came out was a dry, popping crackle.

Terror had seized her, constricting her throat, stifling her voice.

She stumbled backward, her legs threatening to give way.

The man loomed before her. For a long moment, he was still. Then he advanced, his movements slow and deliberate. Though he remained little more than a silhouette in the darkness, Heather discerned a few more features as he drew nearer.

He wore jeans and a canvas jacket. A few strands of hair fluttered in the gentle breeze. He was a little shy of six feet tall; Heather's earlier split-second assessment of the man's height had been correct.

Heather had also been right about the fact that the man was carrying a weapon.

But her assessment of the weapon had been incorrect.

He wasn't holding the Bunny Man's hatchet.

He held a machete.

As his boots crunched on the forest floor, the blade momentarily caught the faint starlight. It glistened.

It was then that Heather's voice returned.

She screamed.

## CHAPTER TWO

*Sioux City, Iowa*

LIFE THROWS many obstacles in the path of a vigilante assassin. Most of them are predictable. Many aren't. Sometimes, even a shopping cart can prove to be a mission hindrance.

Silence Jones prowled the dimly lit alleyway, suppressed Beretta 92FS at the ready. Senses heightened. Muscles taut. Gusts of wind howled through the narrow passage, tugging at his hair, stinging his eyes, and whipping at his clothing—a Banana Republic light gray henley T and a pair of five-pocket dark blue twill trousers. The strong winds kicked up the debris scattered around the alley, swirling up a mixture of paper scraps, leaves, and clanking soda cans.

Silence pressed forward. He narrowed his eyes against the assault of windblown particles and scanned the surroundings. Somewhere within this maelstrom was Lawrence Gaudet, the perpetrator of an unspeakable act.

As Silence continued, he became aware of an unsettling noise, something piercing through the howling wind—a distant rumble, growing louder. He turned just in time to catch sight of a runaway shopping cart hurtling down the alley toward him, propelled by the gale-force winds. It was rusty, bent up, with a mound of debris in its basket, and it careened madly, bouncing off walls and rattling with the force of its own momentum.

Without hesitation, Silence's massive but lithe figure juked to the side, channeling one of the many disciplines in which he'd been trained: Capoeira, an Afro-Brazilian cultural practice that blurs the line between combat and dance. The chaotic cart barreled forward, its ruined rubber wheels screeching against the pavement, seemingly locked onto Silence's position.

Right as Silence slapped a palm onto the nearest brick wall and rotated his torso in completion of the Capoeira maneuver, the cart rattled past, missing him by a hair's breadth. As Silence finished his revolution, his chukka boots crunched on the ground, bringing him to a halt. He watched as the shopping cart continued its wild journey. Before it disappeared into the darkness, he saw that the load in the cart's basket was a tangle of copper wire.

Copper was frequently stolen because of its high scrap value, getting snatched from construction sites, railroads, and vacant homes. A theory about the shopping cart quickly formed in Silence's mind.

He resumed his progress, eyes fixed on the path ahead as the wind continued its relentless assault, echoing off the walls, a haunting symphony of howls and whistles. Its invisible hands pushed and pulled at him.

He rounded a corner and caught a glimpse of Gaudet disappearing into the distance. The man was short and stocky, with pale skin and a head that was mostly bald, with thin strands of gray hair that hung limply down his neck. As

Gaudet turned into a side alley, he glanced back in Silence's direction. His beady eyes glinted in the darkness.

Silence raced after Gaudet, his footsteps blending with the noise of wind and debris. The alley stretched before him endlessly. Silence gritted his teeth. He knew where Gaudet was going, why the creep had taken that particular right turn. It led to a major street, opening up to the grid of downtown Sioux City and the crowds of the Midnight Market Bazaar—an eclectic market that came to life after dark, filled with vendors selling unique crafts, art, and food from around the world. After a few hours of deliberation, the bazaar's organizers and the Sioux City Chamber of Commerce had decided to maintain the event as scheduled, despite the windstorm, so now, both 5th and 6th Streets were closed off from automobiles and packed with foot traffic.

Gaudet would vanish into the crowd if Silence didn't close the gap.

Silence's contact—Fred "Slick" Chambers—had warned him of Gaudet's dangerous nature. Gaudet was no ordinary adversary. The man had sunk into an emotional storm of resentment and obsession, becoming a looming specter in Sioux City. His abhorrent crimes were rooted in the echoes of a failed marriage that had been poisoned by a mix of the usual suspects of infidelity, money issues, greed, and jealousy. All of Gaudet's victims were related to his estranged wife—cousins, second cousins, a sister-in-law.

For days, Silence had meticulously tracked the elusive Gaudet through Sioux City. Now, the time for confrontation had arrived, but if he didn't act swiftly, it could slip away.

Gaudet suddenly reappeared, bolting around the corner in Silence's direction. In a fraction of a second, Silence both raised his Beretta and lowered it.

Because the man *wasn't* Gaudet.

He was a vagrant—tattered coat, weathered cheeks,

sunken and weary eyes, greasy hair whipping in the wind. His face registered panic, and Silence recognized that the expression wasn't simply a reaction to the fact that a pistol had been aimed at him for a fraction of a second.

Silence gestured in the opposite direction.

"It went that way," Silence said and swallowed.

The vagrant's eyes widened for a moment at the sound of Silence's voice—a ruinous, terrible grumbling that sounded mechanical and volcanic and hardly human. Whenever someone heard the unfathomable sound for the first time, the person couldn't help but react.

The voice wasn't just a hideous thing to hear; it was also painful. An incident years earlier nearly killed Silence and left him with a permanently damaged larynx. Speaking was torturous to the mass of scar tissue in his neck, and the more syllables he used, the more intense the torment, so he had to swallow frequently to lubricate his throat.

After the momentary paralysis, the vagrant nodded.

"Thanks, brother."

He continued past Silence, running in the direction Silence had pointed to retrieve his errant shopping cart full of valuable copper.

Silence was a man who righted wrongs for a living, so he would never help someone commit theft. But he had no proof that the man had stolen the copper—no matter how probable that scenario was—and the vagrant looked like he needed a helping hand. So Silence had no qualms about pointing the guy in the direction of his missing cart.

Silence sprinted, closing the gap to where he'd last seen Gaudet. As he rounded the bend, he found his target again, halfway down the latest alley, taking another turn, only yards from the street and the noisy crowd braving the weather and the festival tents shaking in the gusts of wind. But there was something in the way, a literal roadblock at the end of the alley—a ten-foot fence. Gaudet made it to the barrier and sprung upon it with a frantic leap. He scrambled up the chain link.

This gave Silence an opportunity.

Silence sprinted up to the fence as Gaudet neared the top. His hand clasped around Gaudet's left ankle while his other hand grabbed the fence. Gaudet kicked hard and fast with his free foot, smashing the sole of his boot into Silence's face. A sharp stab of pain shot through Silence, out of his skull and into his ruined throat. But it did nothing to shake him. He yanked Gaudet from the fence and sent the man's chubby body crashing to the ground.

Gaudet yelped at the impact, and this noise immediately strengthened into a reactionary shriek as Silence descended upon him. Gaudet tried to shuffle backward, but Silence caught both of the man's wrists and tangled his arms into a knot.

"Talk!" Silence said.

Gaudet's little eyes were wide with fear as he stared up at Silence in terror. He knew his fate was sealed. Suddenly, the fright morphed into a sort of defeated confidence. He gave Silence a smug smirk as he stared into him.

"That's right, *I sold them all*," he said. "Half a dozen lost souls, neatly packaged in shipping containers, cast into the wind, never to be found again."

That was all Silence needed to hear. He raised his suppressed Beretta, aimed it at Gaudet's forehead.

"Did Slick tell you?" Gaudet said.

Silence's tensed finger stopped just in time, releasing the pressure on the trigger. He lowered the barrel slightly, looked at Gaudet, waited.

Gaudet sneered broader. "That's right. Nexus is the real reason—"

Sirens.

Both Silence and Gaudet turned to look. In the distance, past the mass of people on 6th Street, were blue lights. A squad car's door opened, and a cop stepped out and bounded in their direction.

Silence turned back to Gaudet's ugly, sweat-covered, smirking face. He needed to know what the man had been prepared to share, the information about Slick and "Nexus," whatever that might be.

But there was no time.

*Crack! Crack!*

Two shots to the forehead. Hot blood spattered Silence's hand, misted his forearm.

A suppressor only does so much to quiet gunshots. The cracks echoed harshly off the brick walls, the asphalt, the trash cans, the dumpsters.

An oozing hole in Gaudet's forehead, a slightly elliptical circle—the work of a pair of bullets in an extremely tight grouping. Wide, glassy eyes stared into the heavens. Mouth agape.

Screams from the throngs on the other side of the fence. People stared in Silence's direction. Through a gap in the crowd, Silence saw the cop running at him, yelling.

"*Hey!*"

Silence took off.

———

Several minutes had passed since Silence's escape from the alley. Now, he stood underneath a set of metal bleachers at one of the festival's outdoor theatre performances, a couple of miles away from the downtown bazaar, which had been shut down after the gunshots. With him was Slick Chambers. The jubilant sounds of the crowd above and around them mixed with the festive ambiance of the play—a plain-language retelling of Shakespeare's comedy *The Taming of the Shrew*—that, along with the whistling wind, created a symphony of celebration that seemed worlds away from the darkness that had consumed Silence's mission.

The adrenaline of the minutes-earlier chase was working its way out of Silence's system, dissipating. He turned to Slick, his contact, and confirmed the grim news.

"Gaudet has..." he said and swallowed. "Been handled."

Slick's usually lively eyes were somber, reflecting the weight of the situation. His only reply was a nod. He looked away.

Fred "Slick" Chambers was average height, several inches shorter than Silence, with a neatly trimmed beard and mustache on a long, pointy face. Caucasian. Pale blue eyes. His glistening black hair—the origin of his nickname—was worn slicked back. He sported a gray coat over a dark blue T-shirt and jeans.

"Before he died..." Silence said and swallowed. "Gaudet mentioned 'Nexus.'" Another swallow. "Mean anything to you?"

Silence was good at reading people—always had been, a helpful skill as an assassin. Based on the glint in the depths of Gaudet's beady eyes when he'd said the word "Nexus," Silence had recognized both Gaudet's sincerity and that there was something sinister to the mystery term.

A sudden change washed over Slick's face, mirroring the shift in Gaudet's expression a few minutes earlier—right before he'd mentioned "Nexus," moments before Silence had put two bullets in his head. Slick's demeanor turned snide, and a smirk played on his lips.

"This 'organization' of yours did all the digging on Gaudet, right?" Slick said. "They verified everything from my research, found out that Gaudet was the only person who could have abducted those females?"

Silence didn't immediately respond. Slick had evaded his question with a question—a move perfectly befitting a wayward attorney—and that snide look on the man's lips was so eerily similar to Gaudet's that it was making the hairs on Silence's forearms stand up.

But he needed to keep Slick talking. And he needed to reassert the righteousness of his employers, the Watchers, a secretive organization embedded within U.S. government who surreptitiously and illegally conducted their own investigations and sent out assassins like Silence—called Assets—to correct procedural injustices, doling out death sentences to those who truly deserved them.

"Of course..." Silence said and swallowed. "We're always..." Another swallow. "300 percent sure before..." Another swallow. "We pull a trigger."

Silence narrowed his eyes. He took a step closer to Slick.

And Slick took a step backward, going toward the gap between the pair of creaking bleachers towering above them. He continued to grin through that beard of his.

An empty paper Coca-Cola cup whooshed past, clattering disproportionately loudly on the ground as it shot between them and disappeared into the darkness beneath the bleachers.

"Good," Slick said. "Then you've no need to worry about what you've done."

He continued backward.

Silence followed.

"What's 'Nexus'?" Silence said in a growl, allowing his ruined throat to emit its crackling tone to its fullest, creepiest, and most intimidating, despite the pain.

"I'm afraid I lied to you about a couple of things," Slick said, still moving backward, still grinning, still avoiding Silence's question. "I didn't know any of those girls. And I didn't stop in Sioux City for pro bono work."

Slick was almost to the crowd. He was out of arm's reach, but Silence was deadly fast; he could rush forward and snatch him.

...if it weren't for the crowd.

Slick was almost there.

A boy holding a pinwheel—that spun like mad in the wind —pointed in their direction and said, "Look, Mommy! There are men under the seats!"

Slick abruptly turned and bolted, pushing his way through the crowd.

Silence took chase.

He tramped through the horde, his feet light on the ground as he navigated around the people who watched him with confusion and anger; his presence had disrupted their Shakespeare. He kicked over a lawn chair that someone had left behind, creating a yard's worth of clear passage.

Slick was ahead. Moving rapidly. The man stole a glance over his shoulder. Their eyes locked for a moment.

Slick sprinted toward the stage. Performers in garish outfits shone brightly under the artificial lights, belting their dialogue. The crowd laughed.

Silence lunged past a wagon loaded with a blanket, a wooden basket, and a bottle of wine. He was within yards of Slick.

But before Silence could make it any closer, Slick grabbed a metal scaffolding holding one of the massive lights positioned at the corners of the theatre stage. He yanked, and with a metallic creak that carried over the wind, it toppled over.

The screaming crowd scattered, clearing a path for the structure as it crashed into the pavement. The light exploded with a blaze of sparks, followed by a fire that filled the air with smoke and panic.

The crowd shrieked and ran in all directions, and Silence

quickly lost sight of Slick amidst the chaos. He searched desperately for any sign of the man but couldn't find him anywhere in the sea of people fleeing the area.

Silence stopped. He gritted his teeth.

As the cacophony of noise washed over him—the screams, the footfall, the wind—the crowd bashed against him from all sides. But he stayed rooted where he was, contemplating the gravity of the uncertain path ahead.

Years ago, at the beginning of his tenure as a Watchers Asset, he'd quickly understood that his work as an assassin would be full of unexpected twists and turns. But some twists and turns were more unexpected than others.

Moments such as this...

Being double-crossed by a client...

*A client!*

As his teeth gritted tighter, his fists clenched too. He felt his mind falling into a dark loop, something that happened when his often tumultuous brain space became overwhelmed. In events like this, the voice of his murdered fiancée, C.C., came to him to quell the confusion.

She spoke to him now.

*Love*, she said.

*Yes?* his mind's voice replied.

*Calm.*

*But he double-crossed us!* Silence said. *He used us to kill Gaudet for him, and I don't even know why!*

*Calm yourself, love.*

*Slick doesn't even have an address. He's a high-class drifter. He—*

*Love!* C.C.'s voice shouted. *Shhh. Close your eyes.*

She was telling him to meditate.

*No, C.C. Not now.*

*Close your eyes.*

Silence groaned. But he acquiesced, shutting his eyes.

His body continued to jolt left and right with the impacts

from the fleeing crowd, but as he stared into the darkness of the back of his eyelids, the movement became distant, muted, abstract. The harsh wind on his cheeks became a gentle breeze. The smell of smoke lessened, lessened, lessened until it was gone.

Silence opened his eyes.

A five-second meditation.

His mind felt better. *He* felt better.

C.C. was right. She always was.

*Thank you*, he said in his mind.

*You're welcome.*

C.C. left.

Silence turned against the flow of the crowd and trudged away. The darkness that had been Lawrence Gaudet had been extinguished, but a new darkness, shrouded in confusion, loomed on the horizon.

# CHAPTER THREE

*Pensacola, Florida*

Five days later.

Silence took another sip of water before he continued reading the book aloud. He sucked in a breath, delaying even more, knowing what part of the book came next.

Finally, he proceeded.

"'As he placed a strong, calloused hand...'" Silence read and swallowed. "'On the curve of her hip...'" Another swallow. "'Lady Vivienne's nipples came to life...'" Another swallow. "'With a tingle. Her mind went mad with...'"

He reached out for the glass of water on the table in front of him, and a set of tiny, wrinkled, dry fingers took his forearm, giving him a gentle squeeze.

"That's enough, Silence," Rita Enfield said in her withered voice. "Your throat needs a break."

*Oh, thank God.*

Silence took a sip and closed the paperback.

By now, Silence knew the story by heart—the tale of an impetuous young royal who falls in love with a commoner and faces a plethora of melodramatic consequences. He even had long passages memorized word for word. He had read this romance novel—*Kingdom of Desire*—to his blind, elderly neighbor many times over the years. This ritual was a multi-month affair, given Mrs. Enfield's insistence—in respect for Silence's painful throat—that Silence read the book to her in fifteen-minute intervals.

Mrs. Enfield listened to copious audiobooks, mostly on tape but also, recently, on CD, having been introduced to the wonders of digital discs via her former caretaker, Lola. But *Kingdom of Desire* had long been out of publication, and it had never gotten the audiobook treatment. And though it was an obscure title, it was Mrs. Enfield's favorite book and an important part of the old woman's life.

That's why Silence had read it to her in his awful voice so many times.

So, so many times.

Despite the novel's love scenes being PG, fade-to-black affairs, they were just salacious enough to make Silence uncomfortable when reading them to his ancient neighbor. He particularly loathed the moment when Tristan took Duchess Vivienne into his arms outside the horse stables just before the scene cut out, alluding to a literal roll in the hay.

Describing Lady Vivienne's nipples to Mrs. Enfield was the worst part...

He placed the glass of water back on the table and looked at her. Mrs. Enfield sat silently in her chair, where for the last fifteen minutes, she'd listened intently despite the frequent interruptions.

He found Mrs. Enfield's milky white, lifeless eyes looking at him. She was smiling serenely, and her hands were stacked on her lap—a mound of dark, dry skin atop her faded cornflower blue dress. She was tiny, black, frail, and had hair even whiter than her functionless eyes. Her feet barely met the floor from her position seated in the claw-foot chair.

Mrs. Enfield's Victorian-era house had the potential to be stunning, but its antique quality, along with the woman's outdated furnishings, along with the fact it was always rather dark—it *was* a blind lady's home, after all—created an atmosphere that Silence had always found unsettling. Fortunately, Mrs. Enfield had the windows open to their screens, letting in some fresh morning air before the heat and humidity of the afternoon, and this illuminated the place more than usual.

Silence closed the book and placed it on his right thigh. His other thigh was occupied. Baxter—a massive and perpetually peaceful orange tabby—had the front half of his considerable girth stretched across Silence's leg; the cat's rear end filled the opposite side of the musty loveseat.

As Silence glanced down, Baxter immediately looked up. The cat's purring grew louder when their gazes met, and his golden eyes squinted with contentedness. A string of drool dangled from the corner of Baxter's mouth, glistening in the morning sunlight. He drooled constantly. For once, the drool had spared Silence's pants; instead, it had formed a small pool on the loveseat's antique upholstery.

Silence ran his fingers over the well-loved paperback and studied the cheesy painting on the cover. The ruggedly handsome Tristan sported a simple white tunic, dark trousers, and boots. Lady Vivienne wore a golden gown with intricate beading and a lush velvet train. Both of them had long hair that floated via some sort of ethereal breeze amid their passionate, forbidden encounter. Bodies entwined. Lips nearly touching. Longing and defiance smoldering against a backdrop of a majestic castle. *KINGDOM OF DESIRE* was emblazoned in elegant gold script across the top.

"Thank you, Si," Mrs. Enfield said, her withered voice full

of warmth as she settled back into the armchair. Her eyes closed as a reminiscent smile came to her face. "Rory would sit right where you are and read to me for hours. He read *Kingdom of Desire* even more times than you have. I do love that book."

Silence again glanced at the cover, focusing on the model's faces, their exaggerated desire and intensity. At first glance— or upon first reading—*Kingdom of Desire* didn't seem like a book that would hold a special place in anyone's heart. To Silence, it seemed rather throwaway, like something even the author herself had forgotten about as soon as she'd written it.

But people get sparked by quirky things, and something about *Kingdom of Desire* had sparked something in Mrs. Enfield when she was a twenty-something-year-old young woman, so much so that her husband had continued to read it aloud to her when she went blind in her thirties.

Years later, long after Rory had passed, Mrs. Enfield's caretaker, Lola, began reading the book to her. Silence moved in next door to Mrs. Enfield shortly after Lola left Florida, so the *Kingdom of Desire*-reading torch had been passed on to him, a chore he'd dutifully tackled for years.

Mrs. Enfield's eyes were still closed, her lips still upturned in a contented smile. "And I surely loved that man."

With the notion of Mrs. Enfield's deceased husband, Silence's attention went to the accent table by the stairs. He saw a framed picture of a much younger Mrs. Enfield and Rory—a bulky African American man with a warm smile, a mustache, and a shaved head. It was a candid photo, taken in a park, black-and-white. Arms wrapped around each other. Fully in love.

Mrs. Enfield was tiny even in those days, not in an eaten-away-by-time manner, but in a petite way. The photo had been taken only a couple of years before she went blind, and her eyes were clear and alive on a beautiful face.

A few inches away from the photo of Mrs. Enfield and Rory was another framed photograph.

*That* photograph.

It sat in a pewter frame. Lola had taken the photo at Mrs. Enfield's request a few years ago. Centered in the frame, filling up nearly the entire image, was Silence. He sat upright in one of Mrs. Enfield's grotesque old chairs with Baxter on his lap. The cat was looking right out of the photograph, happy as can be, drooling on Silence's trousers. The cat's smile was larger and entirely more genuine than Silence's, whose smile was actually a thinly veiled grimace of bewilderment from the awkward situation: being posed with a cat on a creepy old chair for a photograph taken for someone who couldn't see.

A flashing light by the frames and beneath the lamp caught Silence's attention—Mrs. Enfield's answering machine. A blinking red *1* indicated an unread message.

"Silence," Mrs. Enfield said. "You haven't been acting right since you got back."

How did she always know when something was up?

Silence didn't respond.

"What is it?" she insisted.

Silence thought back to Sioux City, putting two bullets through Lawrence Gaudet's face. As always, Silence had been entirely sure that the man deserved a vigilante execution. Watchers Specialists had confirmed and reconfirmed that Gaudet was the only person who could have abducted the women and girls. Gaudet had even confessed to the act—with sneering defiance—just before Silence squeezed his trigger.

A handful of Assets had been dispatched across the country and worldwide to find the missing females. Silence's part in the operation was over, and he had complete confidence in his contemporaries, despite being faceless and nameless to him due to Watchers protocol.

Though Silence's Sioux City mission was completed, the investigation was open-ended. With Fred "Slick" Chambers's cryptic admission to double-crossing Silence, followed immediately by his violent disappearance, Watchers Specialists were investigating where the drifter might be and what "Nexus" might mean.

Yet it wasn't the procedural open-endedness that was bothering Silence; it was the fact he'd been bamboozled. Slick had portrayed himself as a well-meaning person, someone in over his head and needing an outside force to help him bring justice to Lawrence Gaudet.

But he'd lied.

The fact Silence had misread Slick—despite Silence's potent ability to read people—was eating at him.

Eating him alive.

Mrs. Enfield was good at reading people also, and she'd noticed for the last several days since Silence's return from Iowa that something was wrong. Silence couldn't tell her about Slick even if he wanted to—which he didn't—due to the secrecy of his work with the Watchers.

"All I can tell you..." Silence said and swallowed. "Is that I was betrayed. Fooled."

Mrs. Enfield nodded. Shortly after they'd met so many years ago, the old woman had perceived that Silence was in a violent line of work, one that he couldn't discuss. Mrs. Enfield was a savvy person, and she knew she shouldn't ask too many specific questions. But she still cared.

"Things aren't always what they seem, Silence," she said.

Silence grinned.

Not only was Mrs. Enfield savvy, but she was also sage. In this way, she was much like C.C.

*Beep.*

Silence's pager sounded. He took it from his pocket, checked the number.

It was Falcon. A Watchers Prefect. Silence's boss.

Usually, Falcon would ring Silence's cellular phone. But when Silence was over at Mrs. Enfield's house, the Prefect chose to page him instead as a sign of courtesy and respect for the elderly woman.

Yes, Falcon knew precisely where Silence was at all times, even when he was only a few feet away from his house in his next-door neighbor's living room...

Silence glanced at his right forearm, at the small scar that served as a constant reminder from his employers. Embedded in his arm was a surgically installed GPS dot that allowed the Watchers to track him at all times.

His attention returned to the flashing light on Mrs. Enfield's console table.

"You have message," he said.

His omission of the A—*You have message,* not *You have a message*—was purposeful. As with his frequent swallowing, using broken English to lower the number of spoken syllables was another technique to help with his throat condition. After the five minutes of reading, he needed every shortcut he could get.

"Oh," Mrs. Enfield said. "Be a dear and play it for me."

Silence eased Baxter off his leg and stood up. Baxter watched Silence leave while he continued to purr, continued to cat-smile. The absence of Baxter's warmth made Silence's thigh feel suddenly cool. He went to the table and pressed the machine's *PLAY* button.

A cheery female voice sounded through the speaker.

*Rita, hello. This is Miss Maven,* the woman said. There was a melodious quality to her voice, one that seemed affected, almost theatrical. *Thank you again for the session. It was so wonderful meeting you. I want to let you know that, yes, I'll be able to make a house call, but with my schedule, it'll have to be in a couple of weeks. I apologize for the delay, but just know that Rory is contented. Talk soon.*

A shuffling sound, then the tape stopped with a click.

Silence was incredibly protective of Mrs. Enfield, and his internal alarms were blaring.

"What was that?" he said.

Mrs. Enfield brought her white eyes in his direction. "Miss Maven. She's a psychic."

"*What?* "Silence said and swallowed. "You went—"

"That's right," the old woman said, cutting him off as she sat a bit taller, raising her chin and rearranging her stacked hands. "I went there yesterday when you were off in town buying more of them fancy clothes or lifting weights or whatever it was you were doing. I knew you'd poo-poo it, so I didn't tell you about it."

"You ... can't drive," Silence said.

"I know how to call a taxicab!" The chin rose even higher. "I ain't *that* feeble. I appreciate all you do to help me, Si, but sometimes a woman's gotta do her own thing, especially when there's a naysayer."

Silence couldn't argue with her assumption that he would have "poo-pooed" her visiting a psychic.

"The message mentioned..." Silence said and swallowed. "Rory."

"That's right. Miss Maven's going to help me speak to my Rory again."

Those internal alarms of Silence's now turned into a blaring set of klaxons. He stepped to Mrs. Enfield's chair and got on one knee in front of her.

"Listen to me," he said and swallowed. "Bad people take advantage..." Another swallow. "Of old people." Another swallow. "And blind people, too."

"Miss Maven's a kind soul," Mrs. Enfield insisted. "I can sense it."

"You invited her..." Silence said and swallowed. "Here, to your house?"

Ever more defiant, Mrs. Enfield said, "That's right."

Silence glanced down at his pocket, the one holding his pager. After returning Falcon's call, Silence would soon be on the road to his next mission, probably within twelve hours. That's how it worked in the Watchers.

Miss Maven's message said she wouldn't be coming to Mrs. Enfield's house until the end of the month. Though some of Silence's missions lasted for weeks, most kept him away from home for only a matter of days.

There was time to fix this.

"About to leave town," he said and swallowed. "We'll talk about this..." Another swallow. "When I'm back."

He placed the paperback on Mrs. Enfield's tiny lap and gave it a pat.

"To be continued," he said before standing up and leaving.

# CHAPTER FOUR

THE HEINEKEN'S cold bubbles were therapeutic to the burning rawness in Silence's throat. He shouldn't have read aloud for so long.

His lengthy legs stretched out before him, one foot crossed over the opposite ankle, next to his glass coffee table. He was leaning back on his sectional sofa—a long, gray, squarish stretch of non-tufted fabric with firm but comfortable cushions. Though the house was several decades old, the Watchers had updated it to Silence's chic tastes when he first moved in years earlier. Silence had had ample opportunity to move out of the house in the years since, but he stayed for Mrs. Enfield.

Over time, Silence had updated the 1955 shotgun-style home even further from the Watchers' initial renovations. Everything was grays and blacks and whites with accents of polished chrome, stainless steel, brushed nickel. Splashes of color came in the form of bright greens—big tropical indoor plants.

Silence had his cellular phone pressed to his ear with one

hand. Held in his other hand was the ice-cold Heiny, his impromptu throat elixir.

"We'll let you know," Falcon was saying. "*Nexus* is a common enough word, and we already have a strong lead on it."

Silence frowned.

"Then why not..." he said and swallowed. "Let me know now?"

Falcon gave a little chuckle, but Silence knew it wasn't as warm as it sounded. Though Falcon was a man wholly committed to good—he was a Watcher, after all—he was also committed to keeping a tight leash on his Assets, as were all the Watchers' higher brass. As such, Silence had grown accustomed to Falcon's avuncular yet underhanded amiability.

"Because you have a new mission, Florida Man. This one's in Jacksonville."

Calling him "Florida Man" was both a benign label and a jab at Silence's Florida residency. It was a dig insomuch as Florida was a quirky place that attracted many quirky people. The "Florida Man" phenomenon was the preponderance of whacky headlines attributed to the Sunshine State—little pieces of unintentional or perhaps semi-intentional humor that were shared nationally and internationally.

*Florida Man Mistakes Alligator for Lawn Ornament*
*Florida Man Claims He Can Speak to Manatees*

Silence was the Watchers' "Florida Man" from a geographical standpoint. Silence didn't know the total number of Assets—since Assets weren't allowed to know anything about their contemporaries—but over the years, Silence had ascertained that there were only a few fellow Watchers assassins and that they were scattered relatively uniformly across the nation. When Silence was first conscripted, Falcon had told him he would work mainly in Florida and the surrounding region. Quickly, however, Silence discovered that this was only a hopeful scenario for the Watchers. As it turned out, Silence had even more missions outside the Sunshine State and its surrounding region than those within it.

"Chelsi Nichols," Falcon said. "You've heard of her?"

"Of course."

Who hadn't? Silence wasn't a country music fan—in fact, not much of a music-listener at all—but for the last six months, it was impossible *not* to hear about Chelsi Nichols. She'd been making waves in the industry for a few years, but this past year she'd broken the barrier from country and exploded into mainstream music in a way that nobody had since "Achey Breaky Heart" with her mega-hit, "Cabin Nights, City Lights," which had catapulted her to superstardom.

"And you've heard about her fans, the controversy over her upcoming tour schedule?"

"Vaguely," Silence said. He wasn't one to keep up with the comings and goings of pop culture.

"Top page," Falcon said.

Taking his meaning, Silence leaned off the sofa and grabbed the stack of papers that had been waiting for him on his fax machine's tray when he got back to his house—mission materials from Falcon.

The top page of the stack was a black-and-white photocopy of what must have been the entertainment section of a newspaper. A large image of Chelsi Nichols—wild curls, beaming smile, bright eyes—covered half the page, top to bottom. The oversized title read, *Sinister Serenade: Chelsi Nichols's Concerts Shrouded in Darkness.*

Silence quickly scanned the article, which outlined the ramifications of two recent murders—the victims were each ticket holders for a Chelsi Nichols concert, slaughtered just before their respective concerts began. Since then, some individuals with tickets for upcoming shows had demanded refunds. Others had demanded that Nichols cancel the remainder of her tour. Others had claimed that the tour was haunted or even that Nichols herself was some sort of super-natural force.

"Flip," Falcon said.

Again taking his meaning, Silence turned to the next scanned page—a crime scene photo. A young girl's body lying in a mound on a forest floor, chopped to bits, blood everywhere.

Silence grunted.

"Two murders," Falcon said. "June 28th. Clifton, Virginia. Heather Winslow, age twelve. Hacked to death in the woods outside her house. She and her mother had tickets to that evening's Chelsi Nichols concert in Arlington—Nichols's D.C. performance for this tour. Flip."

Silence turned to the next page. Another crime scene photo. Another body, this one an elderly woman. No blood this time. She lay on the linoleum floor of a dated kitchen, one leg bent beneath her, arms splayed, eyes open.

"June 30th. Charlotte, North Carolina. The date and loca-tion of the next Chelsi Nichols concert. Also the date and location of another murder of someone with a ticket for the concert. Edith Sinclair. Strangled."

Silence scratched at his chin.

"Murders across state lines," he said and swallowed. "FBI involvement?" Another swallow. "Why us?"

It was Falcon's turn to decipher the meaning. He was accustomed to Silence's broken English, his abbreviated questions.

"Yes, the FBI is certainly investigating, given the murders took place across state lines and threaten to affect interstate commerce. We're getting involved because the FBI isn't taking Chelsi seriously about something."

Falcon left that dangling, tantalizingly so.

Silence didn't respond, just waited.

Falcon continued. "She told them about a roadie, one that left her entourage a year ago, when she was a rising star but before she exploded with 'Cabin Nights, City Lights.' Malcolm Egly. The Bureau looked into it, found a handful of people with that name, none matching Nichols's description. As far as the FBI can tell, this Malcolm Egly never existed. From our surveillance of Bureau correspondence, we know they still have a low-level agent investigating, but it's a nominal effort. They're treating Nichols like a self-obsessed twenty-something sensation.

"Our Specialists, though, think her claims have credence." A momentary pause, and then in a slightly more faux-upbeat tone, Falcon continued with, "That's where you come in. Make contact with Chelsi Nichols, determine if Malcolm Egly exists. If the FBI is wrong about Chelsi Nichols's claims, more people could die. Sort it out. Kill who needs to be killed." Another momentary pause. "The next concert is tonight. Jacksonville. Like live music, do ya, Si?"

"Not really."

"Too bad. Your 'ticket' is in the box."

He said the word *ticket* pointedly, sarcastically.

Silence's eyes flashed to the small cardboard box on the table in front of him. It had been waiting on his porch when he got to his house a few minutes earlier—rush delivery via FedEx.

"Any questions?" Falcon said.

"No."

"Good luck, Suppressor."

*Beep.*

Falcon was gone.

Silence took another sip of his Heineken, feeling the coolness on his sore throat. He placed the bottle on the glass table in front of him and dropped the stack of papers next to it. Also on the table was his latest PenPal notebook. He grabbed it.

PenPals came from the NedNotes company and were spiral-bound with 100 pages of 5 x 3.5" lined paper—compact but substantial. Their plastic covers were available in a range of bold colors. This one was cyan. Silence used PenPals for his copious notes and the written techniques that C.C. had taught him to help him organize his disorganized mind.

One of those techniques was mind mapping—connecting circled thoughts with lines, creating a web-like structure that interconnects various ideas. Silence pulled the mechanical pencil from the PenPal's spiral binding, scribbled out a quick mind map for his new mission, then snapped the notebook closed and dropped it back onto the table.

Next to where the PenPal landed was the small cardboard box, its top flaps steepled open after Silence had perused its contents just before returning Falcon's call. He reached inside, felt around, and took out the "ticket" Falcon had mentioned.

It was a lanyard with an ID-holder that held a paper with a sun-and-palm-tree logo and the name *Geissler Music Pavilion* along the top edge. Centered in large type was *EVENT VIP*. Below that, in much smaller print, was *19204*, some sort of serial number.

Geissler was an outdoor amphitheater in Jacksonville, among the top concert venues in the world. Silence had never been, but he understood that it was a massive facility, accommodating something like 15,000 people between the pavilion seating and the sloped lawn area beyond.

Silence ran his finger along the lanyard's edge. To have gotten this access to Chelsi Nichols at the height of the young woman's phenomenon was impressive to say the least. Silence had no clue how the Watchers would have secured such a pass, and that was by design. Assets were left in the dark as to most of the Watchers' logistical procedures.

Being a group of well-meaning individuals embedded secretly within U.S. government, the Watchers had incredible —albeit surreptitious—access to government facilities, infrastructure, and technologies.

Often, the Watchers extended their crafty feelers into the private sector as well, to places like Geissler Music Pavilion.

Silence put the lanyard back in the box and sank into the sofa, crossing his arms over his chest. He looked to the ceiling while allowing his mind to forget momentarily about the upcoming mission. His thoughts were now recorded in the PenPal; they weren't going anywhere. Besides mind mapping, C.C. had also taught Silence how to focus on one issue at a time—*compartmentalizing*, she had called it—and right now, there was another notion playing through Silence's mind, overshadowing the murders.

*Shit.*

Only minutes earlier, he'd found out that Mrs. Enfield was in the grips of a con artist. Now, Silence had to leave her in Pensacola alone to fend for herself. After their brief discussion, it was clear he wouldn't be able to talk reason into the old woman before he left for Jacksonville.

Jacksonville—or "Jax," as it was also known—was on the opposite side of the Florida Panhandle, a five-hour drive across I-10 from Pensacola. Silence didn't need to delve further into his mission materials to know he would be driving, not flying, to Jax. The Watchers had nearly unlimited resources and often moved Silence around the nation via private jets. However, because of the secretive nature of their work, the Watchers had to maintain a low profile. Road trips provided greater anonymity compared to air travel, leading Silence to spend a significant amount of time behind the wheel.

A five-hour travel time was too great to consider swinging back to Pensacola during the mission to help Mrs. Enfield in case of any trouble.

With a sigh, Silence put the notion out of his mind.

And stood up to prepare for the mission.

# CHAPTER FIVE

*Jacksonville, Florida*

Eight hours later.

The sound of the gathering crowd seeped through the walls, portending the energy waiting to be unleashed. Geissler Music Pavilion seated 5,000 at an open-air structure, and beyond that was a sprawling lawn that accommodated 11,000 more general admissions seats.

And the place was sold out.

Chelsi Nichols sat on one of the green room's sofas, looking at the floor as the walls vibrated around her. She allowed her eyes to drift along the pattern of the carpet beneath her sequined cowboy boots, trying to focus her thoughts on her upcoming performance.

And failing.

She was less than half an hour away from stepping onto the stage, and she'd barely even warmed up her voice. The pre-concert tingles she typically felt were gone; in their place was deep-seated worry.

"'In all the places, of all the times,'" she tried again,

singing in a whisper, eyes focused on the carpet's herringbone pattern. "'My heart will be yours for as long as..."

The words faded off.

Again.

She just couldn't do it.

But she would find her voice when she got on stage. Yes, of course she would. She always had.

When she looked up, she saw almost everyone in the room looking in her direction. Chelsi was accustomed to attention, having been labeled a "star" for the last two years. But it was only since "Cabin Nights, City Lights" that she'd been a sensation. Now, even members of her entourage who'd been with her for years couldn't seem to look away.

Staring at her were half a dozen of her security detail, three personal assistants, several Jacksonville police officers, and two members of the Geissler Music Pavilion staff. The Geissler folks were dressed head to toe in black, with comm devices in their ears and clipboards in their hands, smiling at Chelsi. They were the only ones in the room wearing smiles, the only ones displaying any sort of excitement about the upcoming concert.

The scant conversation that had taken place in the green room over the last half an hour had revolved around the recent murders. Each victim had been a devoted fan of Chelsi's, and each was killed hours before one of Chelsi's last two concerts. With just minutes to go before the latest concert, neither Chelsi nor anyone on her staff had gotten word of a murder in Jacksonville. This cast a shadow over both the green room and Chelsi's upcoming performance.

The other people in the room hadn't been bold enough to tell Chelsi their worries, of course, but she'd heard their whispers.

*The killer's going to attack at the concert this time. That's why we haven't heard anything yet.*

*He'll shoot someone in the crowd. With a rifle, would be my guess. What if he's waiting until the concert to kill Chelsi herself?*

They hadn't needed to whisper. Chelsi had been thinking the same things. For three days. Since word had spread of the old woman's strangulation in Charlotte. Thus began the wild speculations about Chelsi's seemingly damned concert tour. That's why Chelsi had insisted on metal detectors at Geissler and the rest of the venues on her schedule. She'd refused to perform without them.

She turned away from the smiling Geissler staff, away from everyone else staring at her, finding the only two people in the room who really mattered—her younger brother, Connor, and Brom Jenkins, Chelsi's primary bodyguard.

Connor stepped closer, tugging at the pant legs of his casual, trendy suit before kneeling in front of her and putting a hand on her shoulder.

"We can't ignore what's happened, Chel," Connor said. "But these fans came to see you." He motioned to the green room, indicating the constant drone of people outside that rattled the framed photos of famous singers hanging on the walls. A quick glance at his watch. "There's only half an hour to go. We gotta get your makeup done. Let's see some of that Chelsi Mae bubbliness."

Connor flashed her a goofy smile—as though coaxing her to do the same—and Chelsi couldn't help but smile back. He had a special ability of getting through to her.

Although they both sported bold, red hair, they didn't look much like siblings. Connor's hair was substantially more orange-ish than Chelsi's, and his face was longer, more stretched out. But he was her brother through and through, with her from the beginning—the *very* beginning, up there on stage with his tiny guitar when Chelsi was ten and he was eight.

Brom looked at Connor, narrowing his eyes slightly, and

stepped beside him, getting closer to Chelsi as well. Unlike Chelsi's brother, Brom remained standing.

"Stay vigilant," he said in his gruff, deep voice, staring down at her with his arms behind his back. "No murders yet in Jacksonville. Something's going to happen here at the concert."

This sent a hush through the green room. Even the Geissler staff stopped smiling.

Whereas everyone had been speculating that something *might* happen at the concert, Brom had just shouldered right through that barrier of hopeful doubt.

But that's how Brom was, and that was one of many reasons Chelsi had selected him as her head of security—that no-nonsense pragmatism, a sort of brutal factuality.

Brom was about five-foot-ten, broad-shouldered with a trim, athletic build. Early thirties. Black. Brom had served in the Army. And though his post-military police officer career had been less than a year—before he decided to change course into private security—he always carried himself with the bearing of a world-weary homicide detective.

Chelsi nodded at Brom, then her brother, then she looked at the carpet again. She wrung her hands as her mind raced. The safety of her fans had always been paramount to her, and the recent murders had shaken her to her core. So many people had tried to get her to cancel her concerts—not the least of which were members of the press—while there were so many others who had tried to get her to do just the opposite, to continue with her concert schedule despite the turmoil.

At the end of the day, it wasn't Chelsi's decision—it was that of powers-that-be in higher positions. Aside from measures like the metal detectors, for Chelsi to have any impact, there would need to be lawyers involved, and there would be conversations about broken contracts and failed promises.

As desperation tightened its grip around her, the green room's door swung open, revealing Octavius Osgood, Chelsi's manager. The legendary Big O. A massive African American man with a beard and perpetual sunglasses, whether inside or outside, light or dark. He barely fit through the doorframe as he rumbled inside wearing one of his iconic light-colored three-piece suits—stretched to its limit around his girth—along with a fedora and, of course, sunglasses.

"Chelsi, honey," Osgood boomed in his thick Louisiana accent, waddling into the room. "I feel your pain. I truly do. But we can't let some nut job keep us from what we're supposed to be doin', now can we? I've done everything I can to ensure your safety, along with the venue staff."

At this, he turned and faced the two with the clipboards, who immediately smiled and nodded.

Osgood turned back around, looked at Chelsi, and gave him one of his warm smiles. "Every ticket-holder is being run through those metal-detectors you requested. That should make you happy, right?" A pause. "The show must go on, sweetheart."

Chelsi's eyes met Osgood's, searching for solace in his words. Nothing. Sure, Osgood was doing his best. He always had. But Chelsi's happiness and safety were simply business considerations for Big O.

She took a deep breath, her gaze shifting from Osgood back to Connor and Brom. *They* truly cared. They were her support duo, as different as the two men might be.

But, heartfelt or not, Osgood's sentiment was legitimate. He was right.

*The show must go on.*

With the words resonating within her, Chelsi's trembling hands steadied. She began running the lyrics through her head again, and they sounded clearer, crisper, more true to their purpose.

Yes, it was time to reclaim her stage.

"Thanks, Big O," Chelsi said. "I got this."

Osgood smiled warmly, his eyes filled with pride. "That's my girl."

Chelsi stood and looked at the door. As she did, the group surrounding her parted. For the last two years—especially the last six months—she'd been both unnerved and frustrated with the star treatment. But at the moment, Chelsi didn't mind it. She needed them to clear a path for her; she needed them to get out of her way.

Which was exactly what they had done.

There was a clear route ahead between her and the door that led out of the green room, through the pulsating walls.

With Connor and Brom flanking her, Chelsi strode to the door.

# CHAPTER SIX

OH, now, *this* was a place to murder someone.

The late afternoon sun threw elongated shadows across Geissler Music Pavilion as Malcolm Egly meandered through the vibrant pre-concert scene. The air hummed with palpable anticipation, and it smelled of beer, pretzels, and watered-down soda. There was still a half hour to go before Chelsi Mae was to take the stage, and the place was already packed. Crawling with fans. Thousands of them. Such a joyous energy.

Egly couldn't wait to shatter it.

He was in the grassy field area—the open space for general admission tickets—and ahead loomed the Geissler pavilion, an architectural marvel with a sweeping design. Its sleek lines and open structure created a spacious, modern amphitheater of steel, glass, and wood elements.

Egly's gaze swept across the bustling crowd, so many people proudly donning Chelsi Nichols T-shirts. Among them, Egly's eyes fixated on a peculiar sight speckled throughout the throngs: fans sporting wigs of spirally, cartoonish-red hair mimicking Chelsi's trademark fiery locks.

A grin grew on Egly's face, relishing the opportunity to exploit this fervor.

Indeed, this would be the perfect place to take a life, the ideal spot to send a terrifying message. By causing another gruesome death *here*, right before Chelsi's very eyes, she would have no choice but to take notice.

The first two sure as hell hadn't caught her attention...

He'd begun with the young girl. Outside D.C. In the woods. Egly had chopped her up. The girl hadn't suffered long, but Egly vividly remembered that scream after the first thrust of his machete, how the body had felt as the blade pierced her flesh. She'd begged for mercy, and, in a way, Egly had obliged; the second blow had killed her. She hadn't felt the next blow, or the next, or the next, or the next...

The old bitch in Charlotte had lasted longer. In fact, she'd put up a hell of a fight. For a few moments, Egly had even thought the hag would squirm out of his grip. She'd socked him a good one right across the jaw, and Egly had nearly lost her. But just before she could get away, Egly grabbed both of her ankles, bringing her crashing down to her kitchen's black-and-white linoleum. Finally, Egly got into a winning position, right behind the old woman. The body had flailed against him as she gasped for breath. She thrashed. The rubber soles of her shoes squeaked on the floor. And suddenly, she was still.

But Chelsi hadn't been impressed. Sure, she'd made statements to the press. Teary-eyed pleadings. She'd given her sincere condolences to the victims' families and friends. But Egly hadn't been contacted. Days had passed. His cellular phone had remained silent. His P.O. box had been empty.

It wasn't supposed to happen this way.

He was to have heard from her by now. He was to have told her he was the killer. This confession would stun Chelsi, naturally, and at first, she would be frightened. Soon, though, she would be impressed, especially after he told her he killed the people solely for Chelsi's favor. Women love bad boys. And the badder the boy, the better. Richard Ramirez, "the Night Stalker" serial killer, received love letters after his incarceration. So did people like Ted Bundy and Charles Manson.

To receive his love letter from Chelsi Mae Nichols, apparently Egly would have to keep on killing. The thought of this made his cheeks flush and his lips curl. Chelsi should *already* recognize him for the genius he was. She should be in awe of his work. She should both fear him and ache for him.

While the venue gradually filled to near-capacity, the energy pulsating through the air continued to grow. Conversations buzzed with excitement, laughter, and eager anticipation. On the cusp of surrendering to the approaching dusk, the sun bathed the surroundings in a warm golden glow as the shadows grew even longer.

His gaze fell to the east, out of the bright setting sun, to one of the ornamental metal towers scattered across the venue. It was maybe twenty feet tall and made of vertically arranged metal rods painted bright orange-red. At its apex, the rods were twisted in giant loops—artistic representations of Chelsi's famous curls.

In the distance, past the tower, Egly's eyes were drawn to a different structure—a dedicated platform meticulously arranged to accommodate individuals with disabilities. Rows and rows of people in wheelchairs.

Egly headed east.

And his grin widened.

# CHAPTER SEVEN

SILENCE COULD SEE the crowd from the highway. Hell, he probably could've seen it from space.

The art-gallery-worthy pavilion was surrounded by thousands of people reveling in the late afternoon's dying sunlight. Silence sensed the throngs' anxious energy all the way from his position on Jacksonville's I-295 beltway. He flicked on the turn signal and took the exit, immediately coming to a stop. Red taillights before him. A line of traffic creeping down the ramp.

As he rolled to a stop, he took his right hand from the leather-wrapped steering wheel and rested it on the gear selector. The car was a silver Mercedes SL class. He'd had it for four months. The Watchers swapped out their Assets' brand-new vehicles every six months.

He'd been listening to his supplemental mission materials, but now that he was at a standstill, he had a chance to use his eyes as well. He turned to the passenger seat. There, propped up, was an eight-inch electronic screen atop a VCR. The screen was a so-called "tablet," one of the Watchers' next-century, not-yet-available-to-the-masses tech. Projections indicated that someday tablets would be everyday devices for use with digital video. As it was now, though, the Watchers had extended their resourcefulness to bring the future and the present together.

Hence the VCR.

Silence had the bulky device connected to the sleeker one via a set of RCA cables. He was powering the VCR via the Mercedes's cigarette lighter and one of the Watchers' power converters.

It was an ungainly eyesore of a setup, but it got the job done.

Earlier, Silence had found a VHS tape—along with the lanyard—inside the cardboard box awaiting him on his front porch. He was watching the tape now.

The new-meets-old combination sitting on Silence's passenger seat wasn't perfect, and the tablet converted the VHS tape to a heavily pixelated image. But Silence still discerned Chelsi Nichols and her wild red hair and beaming smile sitting at an angle, legs crossed, fielding questions with broad nods of the head and swings of the arms. It was the end of her *Present Day* feature from a month earlier. The off-screen interviewer, Vanessa Wheatley, "America's Voice of Reason," offered a final question.

"So what does the future hold in store for Chelsi Mae Nichols?" Wheatley's stately yet calming voice said.

Ahead of Silence, the brake lights relented, and traffic crept forward, nearing the end of the ramp. He put the Mercedes back into gear and progressed. After a few yards, he came to a stop again.

Chelsi turned her head in a show of over-the-top concentration. She twisted her lips to the side. Her wild curls swayed and bounced.

"You know, Vanessa, I'm living life as it comes, enjoying every moment," Chelsi said in her Mississippi accent before looking right at the camera. "And I just can't thank y'all enough for giving me this life."

A new camera angle revealed another pixelated woman. Vanessa Wheatley. Sixties. Short silver hair with streaks of black. Bright blue eyes. She turned away from Chelsi and squared up to the camera.

"There you have it," Wheatley said, placing her notes to the side before resting her hands on her lap. "From a heavenly-voiced child in Hattiesburg, Mississippi, to a talented teen singing at fairs, to a—"

Static cut Wheatley off mid-sentence. The Watchers Specialist who had compiled the video collection for Silence hadn't been one for artistic editing.

A new clip appeared on the screen. For some reason, the analog-to-digital setup transferred this clip into a less pixelated image than the *Present Day* interview. Chelsi again. Same untamable red hair. Same slightly-over-the-top wardrobe. Same pretty face.

But a totally different demeanor.

Her eyes were downcast. And wet with tears. The backdrop behind her was one of a national news program.

The edit caught her mid-sentence—much like it had just cut off Vanessa Wheatley.

"...well, I just ... I just..." Chelsi faltered. A pause. Her eyes remained downcast. "I don't have the words. I can only say that I feel absolutely terrible for the families. If there was anything—"

Another burst of static.

Then a white screen with a line of block text in the center: *END TRANSMISSION A-23.*

A-23 was the shortened version of Silence's numerical title, Asset 23.

The tape reached its end, and the VCR's blue standby

screen appeared on the tablet with *STOP* in the upper left-hand corner.

Ahead, the procession of vehicles inched forward, exiting the ramp and crossing the street onto the Geissler property. Then, with the squeal of multiple sets of brakes, it came to another stop.

Silence reached over and powered down both the VCR and the tablet. The lanyard was tucked behind the VCR against the seat. He grabbed it and threw it over his neck.

A manila folder caught his attention. Two of them, actually, tucked under the VCR. The top folder contained the printouts he'd gotten from his fax machine that morning. Seeing the folder made Silence's mind flash on the first of the two gruesome photos he'd seen—the mangled child, Heather Winslow.

Silence's jaw clenched at the mere thought of the image. Of course, the other crime scene photo was awful, too—*any* murder was tragic—but when a child fell victim to violence, it always amplified Silence's disgust to a raging boil.

When Silence found the person who did this, he would simply ask them *Did you kill the child?* If the answer came in the affirmative, Silence would skip any further protocol and end the mission right there.

With two bullets to the person's face.

While the top folder contained the gruesome photo of Heather Winslow—as well as that of the other victim, the elderly woman, Edith Sinclair—the bottom folder was also tugging at Silence's attention.

He lifted the VCR and pulled out the lower folder, leaving his current mission materials behind.

Inside the folder were the printed materials from Silence's previous mission. The mission he'd wrapped up five days earlier. The one in Sioux City. The one that the Watchers had deemed a success. The one that was closed.

A full-sheet photo stared up at Silence as soon as he flipped open the folder. Slick Chambers. Pointy face. Neatly trimmed beard. Slicked-back hair. There was a sparkle in Slick's eyes, one that Silence had initially misidentified as an attorney's coy twinkle. Really, it was something much more sinister.

And Silence, this assassin who prided himself on his ability to read people, had completely missed it. It had flown right under his radar.

The Watchers had told Silence his work with the Sioux City matter was over. But they'd also told him they'd keep him posted on their search into "Nexus."

Being finished with the assignment didn't mean Silence couldn't still think about it. He'd pursued the case materials thoroughly once more and come to a rough conclusion.

Since Slick was a former lawyer who now, allegedly, involved himself in charitable pro bono work around the country, living the life of a well-off drifter, Silence had deduced that Slick must be some sort of extortionist, a swindler, a fraudster.

What the man's specific racket was, Silence couldn't be sure. Perhaps when he learned what "Nexus" meant, he'd have a better idea.

He fished his cellular phone from his pocket, flipped it open, and pressed and held the 2 button for a couple of seconds—speed dial.

A Specialist answered after one ring. Female voice. Tired and hushed. "Specialist."

Silence identified himself by codename and number. "Suppressor, A-23."

"Confirmed. State your business."

"Status update request," Silence said and swallowed. "'Nexus.' The Sioux City matter."

The Specialist groaned. "Yes, Suppressor, we're all aware

of your persistence regarding this issue. We're looking into it, but resources are stretched a tad thin at the moment."

*Beep.*

The Specialist hung up.

Silence collapsed the phone, put it back in his pocket, and took another glance at the open folder.

One more long look into the asshole's smarmy eyes...

Then Silence snapped the folder shut and shoved it back beneath the VCR.

————

A few minutes later, Silence had waved his ID through two layers of security, taking a gravel road around the property's perimeter. The entire time, he was met with a cornucopia of Chelsi Mae Nichols. Everywhere he looked, she was beaming back at him—T-shirts were emblazoned with her face, buttons sparkled with her name, and shelves overflowed with bobbleheads and giant plushies resembling her figure. Families sang her songs. Drunks shouted her name.

The road terminated at a discreet lot at the rear of the property. Ahead of Silence lay an unassuming windowless building—deliberately plain, where performers went to prepare and to take pauses during their acts. This is where he would locate Chelsi Nichols.

There was a single steel door, and beside it was a lone security officer with a metal detector. Earlier, during the drive across the Panhandle, while listening to his spliced-together VHS tape interview montage, Silence had heard that Chelsi had recently demanded metal detectors at all critical points of her upcoming concert venues. This decision was made, of course, after authorities had discovered the link between the two murders. As such, Silence had removed his shoulder holster and stowed his Beretta under the passenger seat.

As he stepped out of the Mercedes, the electric atmosphere washed over him—this sprawling expanse filled with a sea of people, their vibrant energy palpable in the air. The pavilion was just ahead, towering over him, its sweeping angles adorned with pulsating lights that threw a mesmerizing glow across the surrounding crowd. Massive speakers flanked the stage, emanating one of Chelsi's hits.

At the back of the stage was a piece of corporate branding that had become familiar to the world. Chelsi Nichols's logo embodied her country music stardom with elegance and symbolism. Her name, was rendered in an elaborate font with a touch of vintage charm. Stylized nickels at one end were a nod both to her last name and to her humble beginnings, while vibrant red curls at the other end represented her famous hair.

Silence headed for the building.

# CHAPTER EIGHT

"Chelsi, what is going on?" her brother said.

Chelsi stood in the doorway of the green room with Connor and Brom. Her makeup and wardrobe were now complete, her features accentuated, transformed into her larger-than-life stage presence. With these final touches checked off, she had dismissed her entourage, allowing only her two most trusted confidants to remain by her side. This was her ritual, a moment of calm before the creative storm of performing for thousands.

But now, as the backstage atmosphere buzzed with anticipation, Chelsi's pre-concert ritual had been disrupted by knocking on the green room door. Chelsi's trusted men had both given her concerned glances before they both headed for the door. But Chelsi had hurried past them, her cowboy boots thumping on the concrete, and opened the door first—because she had a gut feeling about who had knocked.

The man wasn't what she'd expected. He was tall. Really tall. And big. Really big. Well over six feet in height and broad-shouldered. Dark hair, dark complexion. Sharp cheekbones and angular facial features. It took Chelsi a moment to recognize the similarity she sensed, but she quickly realized the man looked a lot like the actor from *21 Jump Street*—face-wise, anyway, not the man's massive frame. Chelsi had loved that show as a kid.

In the last few days, while anticipating a rogue assistant from the federal ranks, Chelsi had pictured the man wearing a dark suit—by-the-books, bland, bureaucratic. But this guy sported a pair of black chinos, black shoes, and a gray silk Henley with a simple black necklace beneath the placket. Over the shirt was a Geissler lanyard with a VIP pass.

The man said nothing, just looked at Chelsi with a flat expression and blinked his brown eyes as though waiting for her to begin. In his hand was a plastic card.

"You're here because of my speaking to the FBI, aren't you?" Chelsi said.

The man nodded. He extended the card toward her. She took it.

Though it was the same size and shape as a swipe card, its frosted translucent plastic showed no magnetic strip on the back. Two blue design elements slashed down the left side, and blue lettering gave a message.

MY ORGANIZATION IS AWARE OF YOUR SITUATION.

WE UNDERSTAND NORMAL CHANNELS HAVE FAILED YOU.

WE HAVE THE MEANS TO ASSIST.

PLEASE EXCUSE THIS FORM OF INTRODUCTION.

I AM NOT MUTE, BUT SPEAKING IS PAINFUL.

I AM HERE TO HELP.

Chelsi looked up from the card to find Connor open-mouthed. She turned to Brom, standing beside her like a sentry. Brom's skeptical gaze mirrored Connor's, but he said nothing. Instead, his attention was fixated on the card.

The stranger continued to wait, the hallway's fluorescent lights throwing shadows across the severe lines of his face. His expression remained blank yet patient. He held out a hand, palm up.

Taking his meaning, Chelsi returned the card. The man reached into his back pocket, took out a wallet, and put the card away.

"Your 'organization,'" Chelsi said. "It's not the FBI?"

The man shook his head.

She waited for further explanation. None came.

"What's your name?"

"Zack."

Chelsi stepped back. Beside her, Connor and Brom stirred. Connor gasped.

Zack's voice was shockingly deep and crackling. Just awful. Almost unreal.

Still robotically patient, Zack continued to stare as the confusion washed over Chelsi's trio.

"Chelsi..." Connor uttered.

She turned to him. Her brother gave her a stern look. She ignored it and returned her attention to Zack.

"Zack who?" Chelsi said.

"Just Zack."

"Who are you with, Zack? What 'organization'?"

Zack didn't respond.

"Chelsi..." Connor said again, pleading.

"Connor, stop!" Chelsi said, not taking her eyes off Zack. "But you knew I talked to the FBI ... which means you're connected, but you can't tell me *how* connected you are. Is that right?"

Zack nodded and, as though applauding Chelsi's deduction, offered the tiniest of grins through his stony expression.

"Chelsi!"

She spun on her brother to find him glowering at both her and Zack, shifting his gaze between them.

"You have *a concert to perform*. There's no time to play Nancy Drew with some mystery government man. The killings have nothing to do with you."

Chelsi looked at him. A moment passed, and she didn't respond before turning her attention in the opposite direction to the more level-headed of her brain trust.

Brom looked down at her with serious eyes, even more serious than usual. And skeptical.

Chelsi glanced between Connor and Brom. Connor's jaw tightened, and Brom's eyes narrowed further, the men's unspoken concern palpable. But Chelsi knew desperate times called for unconventional measures, and she couldn't ignore the flicker of hope that Zack's presence brought.

After a moment of consideration, Chelsi faced Zack again and said, "Come inside."

————

A few moments later, Chelsi was seated on a sofa with Zack sitting on another, a glass table with a flower arrangement between them. Connor and Brom stood on either side of Chelsi's sofa, looking down at Zack.

The green room's walls pulsated with the energy awaiting Chelsi outside. Framed photos of famous performers rattled on the walls. Mirrors lined the right side of the room, and Chelsi caught a glimpse of her garish stage outfit: the sequined boots, perfectly faded blue jeans, sequined shirt, an explosion of purple-and-gold makeup, and the curls.

"Chelsi, we're running out of time," Connor's voice trembled with urgency as he craned his neck to check the clock on the back wall. "We need you on that stage in less than five minutes."

Chelsi ignored him. Across the table, Zack stared at her, waiting. He blinked his dark eyes.

"Talk," he said.

Chelsi swallowed and glanced at Connor. Her brother jabbed a finger toward the clock.

She faced Zack.

"It's Malcolm Egly," she said. "The FBI people wouldn't take me seriously, but I know it's him. I can feel it in my bones."

Zack's brow furrowed. He reached into his pocket and retrieved a small but thick notebook with a bright plastic cover. With a deft motion, he pulled a mechanical pencil from the notebook's spiral binding and poised it above the open page. He looked up, met Chelsi's gaze.

"Who's Egly?"

"Malcolm Egly... he used to be one of my roadies," she began, her words pouring out in a rush. "He seemed devoted at first, but it didn't take long before I realized it was actually infatuation. Always trying to be near me, lingering backstage longer than necessary. It became clear that he was obsessed, so I had to release him from my team."

Zack's pencil danced across the notebook's pages.

"And the FBI..." he said, finishing a note and glancing up at her. "Couldn't find him."

"That's right," Chelsi said and shot Connor a look. Zack's mentioning of this detail further solidified his validity and Chelsi's choice to bring him in, despite her brother's obstinance. "They said that none of the Malcolm Eglys in the country matched my description, nor was there anything in the tax records for his work on my team. Evidently, I had a ghost in my employ."

She shook her head and looked away, contemplating. The sound of Zack's pencil scratching ceased. Then nothing, just the hum of the crowd through the walls. A moment passed. Then she faced him again.

"Eight months ago, I received letters from Egly. Confessing his love. Usually my staff handles fan mail, but I had them stay on the lookout for any letters addressed from a 'Malcolm Egly.' Three letters. All over-the-top. All full of obsession. Of course, I didn't reply. Just as suddenly as they arrived, the letters stopped. I heard nothing from him for months."

She paused.

"Then, five days ago, the first person was killed, the little girl in Virginia."

Another pause.

"I know it sounds like paranoia, but I can't shake this feeling that it's Egly, that he's the one behind all of this. I mean, the fact that there's no record of the man has got to mean something, right?"

Zack nodded.

"Chelsi!"

It was Connor. He stabbed a finger toward the clock again.

Chelsi checked the clock as well. Connor was right.

She stood up. Zack followed suit.

"Brom," Chelsi said, turning to her head of security. "Get Zack one of the security cards. We need him on our team until we get this thing figured out."

"No," Brom said. It was the first he'd spoken since Zack's arrival.

"*No?*" Chelsi spat.

Though she entirely appreciated Brom's protection and his counsel, he'd never openly defied her like this.

Brom looked at Zack, then back at Chelsi. "Your brother is right to be wary. We know nothing about this man."

"I ... I can't believe you," Chelsi said.

"Chelsi!" Connor pleaded, motioning toward the door.

Chelsi scowled at Brom for a moment, then looked at Zack.

"Whether the killer is Egly or someone else," Chelsi said to Zack. "Everyone thinks he's here tonight." She paused to bite her lip. "And I'm about to go out on that stage. I'm going to—"

"I think I know..." Zack said and swallowed. "Where to find him."

Chelsi was too stunned to respond.

Connor and Brom exchanged a look.

And without another word, Zack turned and left.

# CHAPTER NINE

THE SUN DIPPED LOWER on the horizon, turning violet. The surroundings, too, were taking on a purple glow—the vendors selling T-shirts and sun visors; restroom facilities; and all those giddy, anxious faces. Egly surveyed the grounds, his eyes darting from one area to another. Almost time. The audience was brimming with eager anticipation, but Egly's mind was far from the Chelsi Nichols melodies that would soon sweeten the air.

His focus was on the tower ahead, one of those stylistic—yet oh-so commercial, very on-brand—displays of looping metal rods, like sentinels in the crowd. By appearance, the tower Egly was approaching—the one about twenty yards away from the handicapped platform— was no different from the others.

But it's what's inside that matters, as they say.

With a smile, Egly neared the tower. The fading light of dusk added an ominous tinge to the structure, which now loomed high above him. It was several yards across, and as he got closer, he saw all the way through to the crowd on the other side.

But it wasn't hollow. Inside was a stark steel skeleton holding the more decorative, painted rods aloft. In the center was a set of stairs. A simple, padlocked metal door offered access to this interior substructure.

Without breaking stride, Egly reached into this pocket and took out his keys, flipping through the collection to the small one he'd added a week ago. It was clean and shiny, brand-new. He inserted it into the padlock, turned.

*Click.*

The padlock snapped open.

The latch offered a creak when he moved it, and the door's creak was even louder as he threw it open, echoing off the inner structure and the painted rods. As Egly shut the door behind him, he glanced back at the throngs of people surrounding the tower. Only a few people were looking in his direction, and they were only mildly interested. Just as Egly had suspected, his approaching the tower with confidence, not breaking stride when he pulled the keys from his pocket, had made him look authoritative, practiced—just another member of the Chelsi Nichols conglomerate.

Egly's mind buzzed with anticipation of the impending chaos he was about to unleash on this upbeat gathering. The first two carefully planned murders had been pieces of a macabre puzzle, and this third kill would be even more significant.

He climbed the metallic stairs, his footsteps clanging, rocking the entire structure gently side to side. With each step, he was ascending closer to the pinnacle of this mission.

*She* would *see him now.*

There was a landing in the middle and a small platform at the top, a few feet south of the point where the metal rods twisted in massive spirals. On the platform was a gray wool blanket—one of those emergency blankets you keep in the trunk of your car. It was spread open, mounded up in the center. He would retrieve the item beneath the blanket momentarily.

For now, he could spare a few seconds to enjoy the view.

He lowered himself to the platform's diamond plate metal floor, sitting cross-legged. The metal was cold through his jeans. He looked out across the lawn area to the pavilion. Everywhere was teeming with people, buzzing with positive energy.

Egly grinned.

He swept his attention over the crowd—which was now at full capacity—and his eyes locked onto the stage where Chelsi would soon command the attention of thousands. But for Egly, her performance would be a mere backdrop to a bigger plan.

He sighed contentedly.

And reached for the blanket.

# CHAPTER TEN

THE CROWD ROARED. A male announcer's voice had just boomed through the oversized speakers, exclaiming that Chelsi Nichols would take the stage in a matter of minutes.

Energy pushed in all around Silence. Some people were jumping up and down; others were screaming and chanting. Every face was pointed toward the pavilion, but Silence moved in the opposite direction, shouldering his way through the undulating mass.

His attention wasn't on the stage.

It was on those towers.

Fifteen-foot rectangular groupings of red-painted metal rods shooting skyward, spiraling into oversized loops at the top—stylistic representations of Chelsi's trademark hair. Earlier, Silence had detected an inner structure within each tower—a set of metal steps. One of these towers would be the perfect sniper's nest for the killer.

If that loose theory proved false—if the towers *weren't* where the killer had gone—one of the towers would serve as the perfect location for Silence to scope out the scene and find the killer, a bird's-eye view above the pandemonium.

He scanned over the crowd. The sky behind them was going dark, and the scattered clouds were painted in reds and pinks. Against this backdrop, he counted the towers.

Four.

But which one?

The tower to the east was the closest to the stage but also the farthest from the opposite end of the lawn. So Silence headed for the next tower over, the second most eastern.

As he pivoted around a screaming group of female twenty-somethings wearing an assortment of neon Chelsi Nichols shirts, his mind suddenly returned to Pensacola. Despite his work over the years to calm his chaotic mind—using so many of the techniques C.C. had taught him before she was murdered—Silence's brain still flashed sudden distractions to him from time to time.

In this case, he thought of Mrs. Enfield. Alone in her creepy house, sitting in the dark, smiling. In this vision, Mrs. Enfield's smile came as she considered her upcoming meeting with the psychic Miss Maven, which was to happen at the end of the month. Though Silence was confident that he'd be back in Pensacola well before the end of the month, the thought of Miss Maven made his blood boil right there amid the crowd at Geissler Music Pavilion.

He had no idea what Miss Maven looked like. He didn't know how old she was. He knew *nothing* about her. All he knew was that she was a damn con artist trying to rip off an old, blind woman.

*His* old, blind woman.

Silence's hands balled up into fists.

And as his anger amplified, so too did the discordant nature of his brain space. Suddenly, his thoughts left Pensacola, going even farther away from Jacksonville, to somewhere abstract, to a term, a single, mysterious word: "Nexus."

He thought of the call he'd made earlier, before clearing security and meeting Chelsi Nichols in her green room. Watchers Specialists still had nothing to offer about the investigation into "Nexus."

This meant Fred "Slick" Chambers's motives were still unknown, as were his whereabouts.

Silence's fists grew tighter.

He thought of Slick's sneering, bearded face moments before the creep had slipped into the crowd in Sioux City, tipping over a stage light and starting a fire.

Silence wanted to crush that face. Hell, at this point, he didn't even want an explanation. He no longer gave a shit what "Nexus" meant. All he knew was that Slick was no good and that he'd fooled Silence. A fist to Slick's face would wipe away that grin. And then a fist to the stomach, which would—

C.C.'s voice came to him.

*Focus, love.*

Sometimes that's all she needed to say.

Silence didn't even have a chance to thank her before she was gone, already having receded into the depths of his mind.

He was back. The crowd was no longer that of Sioux City; it was a crowd in Jacksonville. The stage wasn't the small, cozy one full of actors in Shakespearean garb; it was a massive, brightly lit one in the distance where Chelsi Nichols was about to perform.

And Silence saw the tower ahead, the second easternmost one, his destination.

He was focused once more.

But just as quickly as he regained his focus, something pulled it away.

Movement.

He turned his attention slightly to his right, to the eastmost tower, the one he'd initially considered but then decided against.

There was something different about this tower.

There was someone inside it.

Silence bolted through the crowd.

# CHAPTER ELEVEN

CHELSI TOOK A DEEP BREATH. As the smiling blonde Geissler staff girl swung the door open before her, light flooded into the darkness, pouring over Chelsi, squinting her eyes. Clutching her guitar, Chelsi took the short set of metals stairs, passed by the smiling blonde, went through the doorway...

...and emerged into a new world.

The crowd roared.

Thousands of them. A cheering, shifting mass of arms and faces and hats and signs that stretched far beyond the pavilion and onto the massive lawn. The enthusiasm radiated like a shockwave. A vibrant evening sky hung over it all, painted in shades of purple, orange, and pink.

As Chelsi's eyes adjusted to the radiance, the sound around her was a deafening roar. She nodded at her band members and waved to the crowd as she strode toward a microphone stand isolated in the center of the stage, waiting for her. Even with everything that had happened, even with the threat of a murderer somewhere out there, she took a moment to marvel at the sight, the energy pulsating through the air like an electric current.

Her gaze drifted toward the towering metal structures strategically placed around the venue. Osgood had insisted that the towers accompany all of her outdoor performances. A bit of extra branding. Osgood was keen on branding.

She thought of what Zack had said...

*I think I know...* He'd stopped to swallow. *Where to find him.*

Her eyes lingered on the nearest tower.

Hmm...

Approaching the gleaming microphone stand, Chelsi felt a surge of energy. Anticipation. Creative animus was shining through, even at a moment like this.

The muse never sleeps.

With a smile on her lips and a sparkle in her eyes, she leaned into the mic.

"Well, hi there, Jax," she said. "How ya'll doin'?"

The response was instantaneous. The crowd erupted in cheers and applause, their collective energy reverberating through the air.

And for a brief moment, an intrusive thought broke through. Chelsi's mind flashed to the figure of Malcolm Egly. Maybe he was lurking through the crowd.

...or, perhaps, climbing one of those towers.

*Focus*, she told herself.

She brought her mind back to the first song she was to perform: "All That You Have," a hopeful and lighthearted little number. Naturally, the crowd most wanted to hear "Cabin Nights, City Lights." But they'd have to wait a little while for that one.

Egly flashed through her mind again.

The memory of his obsession brought a sudden tremor to Chelsi's fingers. She clenched them into tight fists, attempting to quell her nerves.

She pushed the thoughts aside. Fear would *not* consume her. She wouldn't allow it. After all, every person in that sea of faces had passed through stringent security measures, all those metal detectors Chelsi had demanded. She was safe.

Still, a nagging worry lingered in the back of her mind.

She looked at the metal towers again.

And for a moment, she could have sworn she saw someone sitting in one of them.

*Stop*, she told herself. *Just stop.*

She forced the smile back onto her face.

# CHAPTER TWELVE

EGLY WATCHED Chelsi through the rifle's scope as she stood in the center of the stage beneath the pavilion, her figure illuminated by the stage lights. She was sweet-talking the crowd, a little warmup before her first song.

He could just discern the soft curves of her face over the distance. For a moment, he forgot everything else around him —the rifle, his mission, and the thousands of people spread out beneath his tower. The world blurred out of focus until all that remained was Chelsi. He struggled to make sense of the sound of her voice as it melted away into sweet nothingness.

"And I want to thank each and every one of you," Chelsi's amplified voice boomed. "These have been some trying times lately, but..."

The words drifted off. They left. Vanished.

Until it was just the concept of her.

Chelsi Mae Nichols.

Suddenly, Egly shook his head, snapping back to reality. Back to the mission. The mission was Chelsi, of course, so the momentary slip into the ethereal was enough to recenter his resolve.

Egly's face had drifted away from his rifle in his daydream, and he brought it back, placing his eye on the scope. He brought his hand up and put his finger on the trigger.

Then he swung his rifle to the side.

Through the scope, he saw the raised seating area for disabled individuals, the platform he'd spotted a few minutes earlier. A number of the people were in wheelchairs. His eye swept over them as he considered his target. Decisions, decisions.

Finally, he set his sights on an elderly woman in a wheelchair gazing upon Chelsi with a warm expression—a whithered prune of a creature wearing a sweatshirt, a blanket spread over her lap.

Egly grinned.

His finger curled around the trigger...

Tensed...

And stopped.

Something had broken his concentration. Movement.

Egly saw a commotion spreading through the masses below. He tracked it to its source and spotted a figure hurtling towards him with alarming speed, shoving people out of his way as he ran.

For a moment, denial flirted with Egly, an attempt to will away what he was seeing. But then the man in the crowd below glanced up, looking right at the top of the tower, practically making eye contact.

There was no denying it now; the man was coming for his tower.

*Egly had been spotted.*

The man had a muscular physique. His attire was polished, and his Geissler lanyard suggested he was an event official. His sharp, angular face bore a stern expression, and there was an air of assuredness about him. All of this brought Egly to an immediate conclusion: the man must have been a recent hire of Chelsi's, beefed-up security precautions in the light of recent events.

Egly glanced at the rifle. He had a decision to make—shoot the old woman, or put down the rifle and try to escape. He glanced back at the security guard, who was now running full speed toward the tower, pushing through the crowd, people screaming at him.

Shit! The guy was only yards away!

And the man was bringing attention with him. More and more of the crowd members were shifting their focus away from the stage and staring up at Egly's tower. He felt their eyes through the metal bars.

Egly's heart beat faster.

Eyes. So many eyes upon him, peering through the bars. If Egly fired now, they'd all see him. Hundreds of witnesses. Thousands.

He let the rifle go.

*Clang!*

It hit the metal platform, the impact shaking the structure as the noise echoed up and down the stairs.

Now he had to get the hell out of there.

# CHAPTER THIRTEEN

SILENCE PUSHED through the dense crowd, his gaze fixed on the tower ahead. He had spotted movement, unmistakably the figure he had been pursuing—Malcolm Egly. Ignoring the growing panic in the crowd around him, Silence weaved through the concertgoers.

As he neared the door at the base of the tower, Silence's eyes darted to the padlock latch. It was empty. Silence hurled the door open. It screeched on its metal hinges. He rushed inside and quickly assessed his surroundings.

A metal staircase stood in the tower's center, leading to a platform at the top. Silence wasted no time and sprinted towards the steps, his gaze fixed on Egly above, who seemed to sense his pursuit as he glanced down. Their eyes met for a split second.

"Hey!" Silence shouted, his voice echoing through the tower. A shot of pain jolted his throat.

The figure above didn't respond, his focus solely on his escape.

Silence bounded up the steps, his shoes pounding against

the metal surface. But as he climbed, he looked up to see Egly already making his daring move.

In a swift and calculated motion, Egly lept off the platform, airborne for a moment as he flew across the yard of distance to the outer, painted bars. He struck with a *clang*. His palms screeched on the metal, and he yelled out in pain, slipping downward six inches before bringing himself to a stop.

The gaps between the bars were varied with their spiral designs. Egly chose the widest one in the area.

And shimmied through.

He disappeared to the outside.

Silence arrived at the platform moments too late. He threw his leg over the guardrail as Egly had moments earlier, balancing his heels on the scant outer edge. He lept, catching hold of the painted bars a few feet away, his shoes slipping for a moment until he stabilized. Maneuvering himself to the same gap through which Egly had just escaped, he tried to push himself through.

But couldn't.

His shoulders were too damn broad.

Frustration welled within Silence as he looked through the bars and watched Egly disappear into the chaos of the crowd.

Pushing off the bars, he reached out to the platform and could just grab the handrail. He threw his other hand over, swung off the outer bars, and pulled himself over the guardrail and back onto the platform. Bolting off, he retraced his path, going down the stairs, through the door, and back outside.

Emerging from the tower, Silence found himself amidst a sea of panicked concertgoers. The air crackled with tension, and an announcer's voice reverberated through the chaos out of the giant speakers in the pavilion area and the other speakers scattered throughout the facility.

*Attention, ladies and gentlemen. We apologize for the brief interruption. Please remain calm, as our security team is tending to a minor incident. Chelsi Nichols will return in fifteen minutes. Thank you for your patience and understanding.*

Silence's gaze darted to the distant stage, where he saw security swiftly whisking Chelsi away to safety. He scanned the crowd, which bubbled with a mix of emotions. Some people were shouting and gesticulating, while others stood stone-faced. A few were booing. All of them seemed distraught.

Then he spotted him—Egly, fleeing through the crowd like a shadow. Silence took off.

He pushed through the dense, pulsating throngs, his body brushing against sweaty shoulders and flailing arms. The crowd's noise enveloped him, a cacophony of voices rising and falling. Faces blurred past.

Silence kept his focus locked on his prey, Egly, who weaved and darted through the people. Shouts and cheers mingled with the shrill cries of frightened individuals, creating an electric atmosphere that fueled Silence's adrenaline.

Egly seemed to effortlessly navigate the chaos, slipping through narrow gaps between bodies. The bastard was good at this, a natural escape artist.

The crowd surged and swayed, making the chase a constant battle of agility and timing. Silence's heart pounded in his chest. But the people, like an intricate maze, conspired against Silence, shifting and swirling, forming walls that seemed insurmountable. Each time he thought he was gaining ground, Egly vanished behind another cluster of bodies, slipping through the cracks.

As frustration surged through Silence, driving him to push

even harder, he noticed Egly was veering right, going away from the parking lot. The main entrance being in the opposite direction. Where the hell was he leading them?

Silence's legs burned with exertion as he closed in on Egly through the sea of concertgoers. But no matter how fast he ran, Egly always maintained a decent lead.

Finally, Egly reached a fence that separated the concert area from a small, wooded parking lot beyond. He swiftly pressed his lanyard against the electronic device on the gate. A green light glowed, and the gate unlocked, allowing Egly to slip through.

Egly looked back and cast a smug glance at Silence before slamming the gate shut and disappearing past a tree into a row of vehicles.

Breathless, Silence arrived at the gate a few moments later. He hurriedly pressed his own lanyard against the device.

*BUZZ.*

A red light glowed.

He tried the gate. It rattled. Locked.

Another try, putting the lanyard to the metal box.

*BUZZ.* Red light.

And again and again.

*BUZZ.*

*BUZZ.*

The gate remained locked.

Silence looked into the darkness—the trees and the handful of cars, all of them luxury vehicles, even a few limousines.

No Egly.

A bitter taste of defeat mixed with a sense of dark curiosity. How had Egly obtained such an exclusive pass, one of a higher level than even the Watchers had been able to acquire?

For a moment, Silence just stood there.

Then he left.

As he walked along the fence's edge, the noise of the concertgoers enveloped him. Their attention was firmly fixed on the pavilion, and he became just another face in the crowd, not one of the instigators of the recent turmoil.

His eyes scanned the other side of the fence, searching for a glimpse of Egly, but he knew it was a futile, almost pathetic exercise.

## CHAPTER FOURTEEN

CONNOR NICHOLS PACED ALONE in the brightly lit hallway outside the green room. The cigarette in his hand had taunted him for the last five minutes, beckoning him to take that longed-for drag. The facility was non-smoking, of course, and he wouldn't leave the vicinity of the green room just for a cigarette. Not with everything that was happening. Not a chance.

So the cigarette just stared up at him from below, twirling between his fingers, which shook slightly with both the need for nicotine and something a bit more primordial.

His thoughts were far less idle than the cigarette. They'd been racing since the enigmatic figure known as Zack had arrived, and they'd received two more jolts since: first, when Zack left the green room with Chelsi's blessing and once more when Chelsi exited to take the stage.

In the time between the first and second departures, Connor had pleaded with his sister to see reason. She hadn't. Of course. She never listened. That's why all this was happening.

Connor had tried to tell her how reckless she was being,

how bizarre of an arrival this Zack character had made. The sudden appearance of a self-proclaimed helper had set off alarm bells in Connor's mind. He couldn't trust a stranger who materialized out of thin air, seemingly offering assistance but with motives obscured by shadows. The guy had to be a high-level federal operative, one of the unseen hands manipulating the strings that ran the world.

And if Connor's instincts proved correct, the consequences could be dire...

Connor's mind swiftly shifted gears, scrutinizing his sister's actions. Chelsi's naiveté troubled him deeply. Before this recent business with Zack, she'd ventured to the FBI, thinking she could convince them to believe her about her theory of Malcolm Egly being the one behind the killings.

*The FBI! Her! Chelsi!*

She might be famous now, but that didn't make her any less callow. In fact, celebrities were even bigger doofuses than the rest of the population.

Simply unbelievable. Chelsi was blind to the dangers lurking beneath the surface, the potential for manipulation that seeped into every crevice of their lives. And now, she had opened her arms to Zack, welcoming him into their group without questioning his true goals. Connor could no longer afford to overlook his sister's gullibility.

He pivoted at the end of the hallway yet again, going back in the opposite direction. As he wore a path in the floor, memories of their shared past resurfaced, fueling a mix of emotions. Connor had always existed in the shadow of his older sister's brilliance, beauty, and conspicuous charm. Especially the brilliance. There were plenty of cute girls in the world. Plenty with million-dollar smiles, too. But none with a voice like Chelsi's. That's something God-given, something all those other cute smilers could only dream of.

So Connor was merely a supporting performer—first, at

all of those small venues, standing behind his golden-voiced sister, clutching his guitar, and forcing a smile; and now, in the grander theater of her life. He took care of the matters that no one saw, while Chelsi used that voice of hers. Someone had to deal with the concert facility owners, manage the fan club, listen to record label executives' inane demands and musings.

Sometime between his days of standing behind her with his miniature guitar and standing behind her in the bright lights of her press conferences while she fielded questions with her beaming smile and equally beaming temperament, a fog had infiltrated Connor's heart, gnawing away from within. He saw how the world showered Chelsi with blessings, leaving him to grapple with his own unremarkable outcome.

But in this pivotal moment, Connor couldn't afford to indulge his grievances. The world was crumbling around him and his sister, the fragile balance of their existence hanging by a thread. Ultimately, it was Chelsi's fault. *That damn naiveté of hers.* For the longest time, Connor had worked to shield Chelsi from herself, but it had only been in recent times that he realized that he was protecting himself, too. They were intrinsically linked, for better or worse. If she fell, they both fell. Connor wouldn't let that happen.

Which is why he'd taken more aggressive steps lately.

He stared at the cigarette, its allure fading in the face of the imminent circumstances that demanded his attention. With a deep groan, he reached into his jacket pocket, fished out the pack, and slipped the cigarette back in.

Brom burst out of the doorway ahead, leaving the green room, his eyes immediately locking on Connor. He hurried down the hall toward Connor, his muscular figure even more rigid than usual, his eyes more intense.

"There's a situation," Brom said. "Outside."

"*What?*"

Brom pointed to the radio clipped to his belt. "Geissler staff just radioed. Some guy was *inside* one of the towers. Another guy chased him off. Both men disappeared into the crowd at the back. Want to take a guess what the description of the second man sounds like."

"No way…"

"Six-foot-three. Broad-shouldered. Henley T-shirt."

"Shit. Zack."

Connor's suspicions of Zack flooded his head once more. Dammit, he couldn't fathom why Chelsi was so oblivious to the man's obviously disreputable demeanor. There had to be something more significant to this man, this shadow figure.

"The on-site cops already found a rifle," Brom said.

"Shit…"

With a determined nod, Connor followed Brom's lead, and they took off, their hurried footsteps echoing through the empty hallway. The weight of responsibility settled upon Connor's shoulders.

He also felt the much lighter weight of his pack of cigarettes, a slight pressure just noticeable through the thin fabric of his jacket's lining.

Screw it.

He pulled the pack out, retrieved the cigarette that had been toying with him, and lit it right there in the smoke-free hallway as he and Brom stormed off.

# CHAPTER FIFTEEN

LENNY WARD WAS about the biggest Chelsi Nichols fan there was, and he knew every detail of the recent events—the murders and the surrounding controversy. But despite following Chelsi's tour for the last two years—starting before the success of "Cabin Nights, City Lights," when Chelsi was just a star, not a superstar—Lenny never would have thought he'd be a part of the intrigue.

But now, something big was happening in Jacksonville.

He was in the expensive seats under the pavilion. A few minutes ago, while Chelsi was offering her standard warm welcome to the audience, people had craned their attention back to look at something in the distance. Even Chelsi's band members had looked. When Lenny turned around, he had seen something happening in the distance near one of the metal towers. A panic in the crowd.

Then, suddenly, he'd seen a man pop out of the tower and slide down the metal bars!

This was enough to get Chelsi's security into action. They'd flooded the stage, three of them surrounding her, and whisked her away.

A few moments later, as the crowd rippled with nervous anticipation, the announcer had said there would be a fifteen-minute delay. Many people had groaned at this—and a few had immediately left—but there wasn't as much complaint as there would have been at a typical concert. Lenny figured folks were a bit more understanding given the recent murders and the fact that there could be a genuine threat not just to Chelsi but to everyone in attendance.

Now, a few minutes later, things seemed to be calming down. The initial unease dissipated, replaced by laughter and a renewed sense of joy. Lenny couldn't help but smile as he witnessed the resilience of Chelsi Nichols's devoted fans. One group of enthusiastic concertgoers a few rows behind him even began an impromptu chorus of one of Chelsi's beloved songs. Their voices merged, creating a harmonious wave that resonated through the area.

Just as the crowd's spirits began to rise, the male announcer's voice boomed through the speakers, piercing the air once more.

*Attention, ladies and gentlemen. We apologize again, but the break will be extended for an additional fifteen minutes. Chelsi Nichols will return. Thank you for your patience and understanding.*

The crowd elicited a mixed response. Some voices booed in frustration, while others grumbled with disappointment. That patience Lenny had noted only a few moments earlier was evidently wearing thin.

For Lenny, though, something wasn't sitting right. His mind wandered to the events that had unfolded before the concert delay. He recalled the sight of two men locked in a chase, their figures disappearing into the people in the distance before that entire portion of the crowd turned into a panicked swarm. One of the men had scrambled down the exterior of the decorative tower; the other had emerged a few moments later from the tower's base before chasing after the first man.

But it wasn't just the disturbance that was sticking in Lenny's mind—it was the direction the two men had run before disappearing into the pandemonium they created. They hadn't headed toward the back, toward the parking lot and the interstate highway beyond.

They'd gone to the *side* of the facility.

An odd choice...

Drawing on his two years of dedicated fandom, Lenny's mind focused on the Geissler Music Pavilion's layout. He had each of Chelsi's venues memorized—as he tried to know everything, *absolutely everything*, he could about her—so he knew that the eastern area of Geissler, where the men had fled, was a parking lot for the talent and their immediate staff as well as dignitaries and other high-level VIPs.

Curiosity sparked within Lenny, compelling him to act on his instincts.

Excusing himself from his row of seats, he slipped away. His steps were purposeful as he made his way to the edge of the pavilion area to head east across the lawn area.

The night was surprisingly quiet as he walked, the hum of conversations from the concertgoers taking on a mixture of disappointment, nervousness, and malaise. Unsurprisingly, no one paid much attention to Lenny as he made his way across the open area toward the line of trees that marked the fence in the back.

How sad. How very sad that a forty-six-year-old man from Ohio was aware of the existence of a single fence in Jacksonville, Florida, due to his tastes for the music of a twenty-five-year-old woman...

At least, that's what his family and friends back in Lima would think. To them, Lenny was a loser who'd done nothing with his life for two years.

But here was Lenny, walking towards an unknown destination with no clear plan or purpose—taking off toward a fence, going in the direction the two men had just run in some sort of foot chase.

And why?

For what reason?

He didn't know.

But he *did* know that if the folks in Lima could see what he was doing now, they would be shocked.

The farther Lenny moved into the night air, the more surreal everything seemed. Surrounding conversations sounded hollow and distant. The stars shone brighter than ever before. A strange sense of unknown purpose washed over him. This must be what it felt like to take risks, to do something unexpected, to step into uncharted territory.

He had no plan. But for once in his life, he truly accepted the uncertainty of it all.

# CHAPTER SIXTEEN

SILENCE WALKED ALONG THE FENCE, his steps heavy with defeat. Thoughts swirled in his mind, frustration and disappointment gnawing at his insides. And as it did so often, his mind succumbed to the antagonism, swirling into a maelstrom.

Losing Egly made him think of his other recent failures...

Sioux City. Slick Chambers's bearded face, sneering at Silence, an expression not so very different than the look that Egly had shot at Silence right before he slammed the gate in his face.

And back home in Pensacola. Another failure. Leaving Mrs. Enfield alone, her impressionable innocence at risk of a psychic con artist, Miss Maven. If only Silence had caught the signs earlier. Had he discerned that Mrs. Enfield had taken it upon herself to—

*Love?* C.C. said from the back of his mind.

*Yes?*

*Quiet your thoughts. Be gentle with yourself.*

*But I've failed. Multiple times in a row.*

*Oh? Have you? Or have you forgotten what Mrs. Enfield told*

*you back in Pensacola?—things aren't always what they seem. Maybe*
*you need to—*

C.C.'s voice was suddenly cut off by a sound on the other
side of the fence.

*Psst!*

Silence halted, spun to face the fence.

And there was Malcolm Egly.

A few feet away.

With a wicked grin on his face.

Silence's hand instinctively went to his holster...

But it wasn't there. His gun was several hundred feet away,
beneath the seat in the Mercedes.

"Looking for me?" Egly said, his voice dripping with
smugness.

Silence wasn't sure what he'd expected—after all, Chelsi
hadn't offered a physical description of the man—but this
wasn't it. Malcolm Egly was ... plain. Just a guy. T-shirt, jeans,
light jacket. He was about five-foot-ten. Sandy blonde hair,
parted. Caucasian. Thirties. A decent-looking but not alto-
gether handsome face.

The only thing setting him apart was his eyes. It wasn't
their brown hue, but what they showed: a deep-seated malefi-
cence hidden away in the man's depths. Unhinged, yet
unaware. A train without a conductor. A rudderless ship.

Silence's jaw clenched. For a moment, he said nothing.
Then he answered Egly's question with, "Yes."

In reaction to Silence's wild voice, Egly raised one
eyebrow. And that was all. It was a much more subdued reaction than Silence usually received, which made sense given
the man's vacant eyes.

Egly studied him for a moment.

"Who are you?"

"Zack."

"Zack who?"

Silence didn't respond.

Egly's lips curled into a smirk. "You a fed?"

Silence didn't respond.

A moment of nothing stretched between them, tension thick in the air.

Then, in a controlled voice, Silence dared to ask the question that haunted him.

"Did you kill the child?"

"Heather Winslow?" Egly's said, his sneer deepening. "You bet I did. I chopped her up."

Silence lunged forward, his fingers wrapping in the chain link. The fence rattled. Rage surged through him. His grip tightened. The fence shook harder.

C.C.'s voice came. *Love!*

That was all she had to say. She was right. Emotion had overtaken Silence. He took a breath—from the stomach, a diaphragmatic breath. And the tension in his fingers eased. He pulled his hands off the fence.

Egly never budged. He just stood there. Smiling.

"You have high-level pass," Silence and swallowed, pointing to the lanyard in Egly's hand. "A sniper rifle that..." Another swallow. "Got past security." He brought his hand leftward, aiming his point toward the tower. "Who's helping you..." Another swallow. "On the inside?"

Egly's sneer transformed into a knowing smile. "I see. You must be one of Chelsi's, which means you've met the inner circle, yes?"

Silence didn't want to respond to Egly's query, didn't want to give the creep any power at all. But he needed answers.

So he nodded.

"I'll just say that my friend is really close to her."

"Who is it?" Silence growled. "*Talk!*"

But Egly said nothing, only retreated into the shadows.

And was gone.

Silence's mind raced, trying to unravel the meaning behind Egly's words. Breathing heavily, he took a step back from the fence. His heart pounded in his chest as he grappled with the realization that someone within Chelsi's inner circle had betrayed her.

As he walked away from the fence, his mind raced with questions and possibilities.

# CHAPTER SEVENTEEN

SILENCE BURST into the green room. His eyes quickly scanned the space, finding Chelsi standing near the row of lighted mirrors, Brom and Connor at her side. Chelsi looked rattled, her usually composed demeanor shaken by the recent commotion outside. Silence assumed she must have requested to be alone with her two most trusted people in this moment of chaos.

Connor's eyes narrowed as he locked gazes with Silence.

"You! Were you a part of that disturbance outside?"

"Yes," Silence said without breaking stride toward Chelsi.

Connor seemed poised to say something else.

Silence ignored him.

He made his way toward Chelsi, but before he could reach her, Brom swooped over, a glowering expression etched on his face.

Silence paused. While he respected both men's protective nature toward Chelsi, Brom was the only one of the two who posed any sort of physical challenge. He met Brom's intense gaze straight on, but Chelsi's voice cut through before a confrontation could arise.

"Brom, let him be. Please. I want to hear what he has to say."

Silence stepped past Brom.

"I just met Egly," he began, his voice low and intense. He swallowed. "He had rifle."

Chelsi gasped.

"He's... he's here? *Egly?* What do you mean, 'a rifle'? As in a *rifle* rifle? As in a gun?"

Silence nodded.

The confirmation hung heavily in the air, drawing shocked expressions from Chelsi, Connor, and even Brom.

Connor turned to Chelsi, his voice urgent. "That's it, Chel. You gotta cancel the show. It's far too dangerous."

Brom nodded. "He's right. You're not safe if you go ahead with this."

But Chelsi's gaze shifted away from the men, her mind deep in contemplation. Silence could see the weight of responsibility pressing upon her.

Suddenly, her eyes went to Silence as her expression shifted. "Wait ... you said he had a gun. He couldn't have gotten that past the metal detectors, could he? I *told* them to—"

"You're right," Silence said, cutting her off as he took a step closer. He swallowed. "He couldn't have." Another swallow. "You have traitor in your ranks."

"Someone ... someone in my inner circle?"

Silence nodded. "Only explanation."

Brom opened his mouth to protest, but Chelsi silenced him with a stern look.

"You're right, Zack," she said. "We need you on my team." She turned to Brom. "Give him a pass."

Brom started. "But—"

"Now."

Brom glowered at Silence for a moment, then stomped

across the room to a heavy-duty plastic storage cart. He undid the latches, retrieved a plastic card, and brought it to Silence.

Silence turned it over in his hand. It bore Chelsi's logo on the front along with a unique serial code, and, much like Silence's introductory card, the back side was devoid of a magnetic strip. This wasn't a swipe card; it was a contactless card that connected to a terminal via NFC, near-field communication.

He put the card in his pocket.

"I agree with them," he said and swallowed. "You should cancel concert..." Another swallow. "And—"

He was cut off by a deep voice in a thick Louisiana accent that resonated from the doorway.

"No, she won't be doing that."

Silence turned.

Another world-famous person had just entered the room, someone who had been in the public's eye long before Chelsi's meteoric rise to stardom.

It was Octavius Osgood.

# CHAPTER EIGHTEEN

IN THE SMALL VIP parking lot of Geissler Music Pavillion, vibrant floodlights illuminated the surroundings, casting a brilliant glow across the rows of parked luxury vehicles and limousines. As Egly ventured through this haven for the privileged few, the night air crackled with the sound of the anxious concert crowd in the distance.

It had been several minutes since his encounter at the fence with Zack, but Egly had to remain in the parking lot.

For a bit longer.

Until that one special individual arrived...

The crowd's murmurs and restless whispers carried on the wind, blending with the distant hum of a pre-recorded Chelsi Nichols song—intermission music. Egly sensed the crowd's fervent excitement as they eagerly awaited Chelsi's return, blissfully unaware of the twisted dance playing out in the shadows of the parking lot.

Thoughts of Chelsi flitted through Egly's mind, a volatile mix of memories and desires. She had been his connection to this world, his gateway into the inner sanctum of a revered artist. He'd been a roadie. Someone who works behind the scenes. Moving speakers. Winding up cables.

Yes, he'd done those things. But he'd been more than just a roadie to Chelsi Mae Nichols. Their fates had been bound to each other on an inevitable course of tremendous collision. For a just brief moment. These days, Egly was on a feverish mission to correct the errant paths, to bring them back into alignment.

But now, a new figure had emerged, disrupting the delicate balance of his plan. Zack, the enigmatic stranger. A refined brute. Tall, dark, and handsome. Someone who could, in theory, not only derail Egly's plan but also steal Chelsi away.

Yet after their brief interaction, Zack had captured Egly's attention, stirring curiosity and excitement that he hadn't felt in years. In this unlikely adversary, Egly sensed a compelling foil, someone who could match his cunning and challenge his very essence. A thrill coursed through Egly's veins at the prospect of an adversary worthy of his twisted desires.

Above, the night sky sparkled with a blanket of stars, their brilliance enhanced by the absence of city lights, as Geissler was on the very periphery of Jacksonville. They were celestial witnesses to the unfolding drama, their twinkling presence lending an air of mystique to the scene. It was as if the universe itself held its breath, captivated by the forces converging in the parking lot.

Movement brought his attention away from the heavens, back to earth.

Another person was with him now in the VIP lot, on the other side of the space. It was the person he'd been waiting for.

"About damn time," Egly whispered to himself through a dark grin.

He headed toward the other person.

# CHAPTER NINETEEN

SILENCE DIDN'T GIVE a shit how famous Octavius Osgood was, nor how rich he was, nor how influential he'd been in the music industry for decades. He just stormed towards the rotund man, his intentions set.

The dimly lit green room seemed to shrink as Silence closed the distance, tension crackling in the air. Osgood stood tall, his presence commanding as he waited.

Silence stopped in front of the man and took a good look at him. In his line of work, Silence had had more than a few run-ins with celebrities. Up close, they're people just like anyone else. And they look just like the image one has of them in their head, only without the flashy glow of distanced reverence.

Due to his rotund figure and prodigious proportions, Osgood was a pop culture joke fixture. At about six feet tall, he was shorter than Silence, but the round belly—a sort of roundness that would make globes and beach balls jealous— gave him an even larger mass than Silence's formidable size. A slight sheen gleamed on Osgood's dark brown skin, and he smiled, revealing a set of pearly teeth behind his beard. He was wearing sunglasses, despite the limited lighting, along with a white fedora that matched his white three-piece suit.

He was grandiose in a way that only an American promoter could be, and to Silence, Osgood how always seemed like an amalgamation of Don King and Colonel Tom Parker, like someone had tossed the two men into a blender, added a bit of Foghorn Leghorn essence, a dash of Paul Prud-homme, and poured the resulting concoction into a big, round mold.

Like any good American folk hero, everyone knew Osgood's backstory. He was born and raised in the 1940s in vibrant and culturally rich New Orleans, Louisiana, which fostered in him a deep passion for music at an early age. His love for the industry led him to pursue a career as a music manager.

In his late teens, Osgood worked at a local music venue, where he quickly gained experience and knowledge of the industry. He honed his skills in artist management, under-standing the intricacies of contracts, negotiations, and promoting talent.

Osgood's natural proclivity for identifying potential stars and nurturing their careers set him apart. His keen eye for talent and his ability to navigate the music industry's complex landscape earned him a reputation as a successful manager. Over the years, he built a network of connections and estab-lished himself as a respected figure in the music business.

With his thick Louisiana accent and larger-than-life personality, Osgood exuded confidence and charisma. He used his charm and persuasive skills to secure deals, forge partnerships, and propel his clients' careers to new heights. He managed numerous successful artists, guiding them to achieve fame, fortune, and critical acclaim. Osgood's shrewd business sense, coupled with his deep understanding of the industry, made him a formidable force in the music world and pop culture in general.

Neither the man's girth nor his fame intimidated Silence.

"She's not going..." he said and swallowed. "Back on that stage."

Osgood glanced at Silence's lanyard, his eyes narrowing as he took in the unfamiliar face before him. Ignoring Silence's demand, he turned his attention to Chelsi, his voice dripping with displeasure.

"Who the hell's this guy?" he asked, his tone sharp and accusatory.

"Zack. A new member of my security team. I just hired him."

There was a hint of defiance in her tone, but also vulnerability. She had made her decision without Osgood's knowledge, and it was now clear to Silence that this course of action must have been a rarity.

"*You* hired him?" Osgood roared, his body tense.

Silence watched the interaction, his thoughts spinning around the realization of the hold that Osgood's iron grip had on Chelsi's career—and probably her entire life.

Connor took a step forward and said, "I'm with Zack. Chelsi shouldn't take the risk of going back out there."

Osgood slammed his fist into his palm and shouted, "I'm the one making the calls here! She's safe. The cops are coming for the gun, and this guy," he said, pointing at Silence, "chased the creep away. I got *millions* riding on this concert alone."

"Big O, be reasonable," Connor said, shaking his head. "This is *dangerous*. Brom agrees, don't you?"

Connor turned to Brom for agreement.

But Brom wasn't there.

Brom was nowhere to be found.

The weight of quiet settled upon the group, casting a shadow over their already strained situation.

Chelsi hopped out of her seat in a panicked state after losing her top security guard. "Where'd he go? He was just here!"

Osgood lumbered forward, past Silence and Connor.

"Chelsi, my dear. Listen to me." He took her hands. "Who got you this far? You know I wouldn't put you at risk. You're solid gold, beautiful. The gift that keeps on giving. We're looking at a 30-million-dollar year *this year alone*, if we can get past this silly serial killer business." A brief pause, then in a darker tone, he said, "Now put a goddamn smile on that pretty little face of yours and go sing some songs for those slobbering idiots out there. Those are the people making both of us rich. You're needed on the stage in fifteen minutes."

"Okay, Big O."

"Good."

With surprising agility, Osgood twirled his bulk back toward the door and paused to cast a contemptuous glance at both Connor and Silence. He shook his head, waddled away, and slammed the door behind him.

Osgood's patronizing attitude towards Chelsi made Silence want to bust down the door the man had just slammed, chase him down, and smash his fat face into the hallway's cinderblock wall. With a few twisted sentences, Osgood had reduced Chelsi to a mere tool of commerce. However, as the tension in the room eased ever so slightly, Silence's thoughts drifted to Brom, and a piece of the puzzle suddenly fell into place.

A large piece.

He thought of what Egly had said at the fence...

A chilling realization swept over Silence.

Brom, Chelsi's trusted confidant, was the missing link,

Egly's connection to Chelsi's inner circle. Why the hell else would he have suddenly disappeared?

Silence spun on Chelsi.

"You live on..." He swallowed. "The road, right?"

Chelsi's hand went to her chest, and she took a step backward. "When I'm touring, yes."

She gave him a dubious look.

"Your security staff, too?"

"Yes."

Silence thought for a moment. "Where's Brom's locker?"

## CHAPTER TWENTY

EGLY TINGLED with anticipation and delight as he followed the figure he had glimpsed in the brightly lit parking lot. The man's silhouette floated on the other side of the space, tantalizingly out of reach, teasing Egly with each step. Egly grinned. Though the other man had yet to notice him, this was no random encounter—it was a reunion.

With Brom Jenkins.

The name echoed in Egly's mind. Brom. So fitting of the broad-shouldered, dour-faced head of Chelsi's security. Her loyal guard dog. A doberman in a silk shirt and slacks.

A sinister grin spread across Egly's face. He was relieved Brom showed up, as he thought his failure in the concert crowd would make him not come.

But there he was. On the opposite side of the parking lot, strolling past a line of Mercedes, BMWs, and Audis, scanning left and right; he hadn't spotted Egly.

As Egly closed the distance between them, he toyed with the idea of calling out to the other man. But he restrained himself for a few moments. He wanted to savor every memory.

Egly continued to walk behind Brom, a few feet back, through the labyrinthine paths of the parking lot. Each footstep was calculated and purposeful, matching Brom's, canceling out the sound. Shadows danced around them from the bright lights above.

Finally, Egly found himself mere yards behind Brom.

He was going to call out to him, but Brom seemed to pick up on his presence. Slowing to a stop, Brom turned around. His stone-cold face and dark eyes met Egly's gaze.

Egly smiled.

"Hey-a, buddy," Egly said.

# CHAPTER TWENTY-ONE

CHELSI HAD her head down and her arms crossed. She wore a light grey hoodie—which Zack had hastily snatched from her wardrobe—its hood pulled up over her head, obscuring most of her face. Her wild red curls were barely contained under the sweatshirt, and one unruly curl was poking out from the top of the hood. She reached up to push it back in, but it stubbornly remained sticking out.

Chelsi shouted to Zack, "I can't believe I'm breaking into one of my own buses!"

Zack didn't respond; he just kept leading them across the isolated far end of the Geissler property, going to the row of tour buses—massive and luxurious, with glossy black exteriors and glossy chrome detailing that glimmered in the moonlight. Chelsi's name was on each of them, in Osgood's carefully chosen font, with the stylized nickels on one end and red curls on the other. Osgood was obsessed with branding.

"And I can't believe you slipped me out of there," she said, checking her watch. There only a matter of minutes before she had to be back on stage. The crowd's rumble was a low, ever-present roar that echoed in the night air, a nagging reminder.

Somehow, Zack had concocted the plan, grabbed the hoodie, and led her down a series of hallways, eluding her security and that of Geissler ... all in a matter of minutes. Chelsi thought of the vagueness of the message on Zack's introductory card. It had said simply that he belonged to an "organization." Chelsi was beginning to think Zack was some sort of spy.

They took the metal steps up to the bus, the one Chelsi had pointed out when they entered the parking lot. Zack reached into his pocket and took out the security card Chelsi had had Brom give him back in the building.

"Wait," Chelsi said. "Yours doesn't have this level of clearance."

Zack was about to put the card against the black plastic terminal by the door latch. He stopped, put the card back in his pocket, and held out a hand, saying nothing. After a moment to process his nonverbal request, Chelsi handed him her own card.

As Zack took the card, his attention turned to the side. Chelsi looked too. Past the fence, in a gap between the trees, was the silhouette of a robust man. He wasn't at Osgood's level of girth, but he was a big guy, and he was clearly watching them. When a moment passed, the man must have realized he'd been spotted because the silhouette moved away, disappearing into the shadows.

Zack placed Chelsi's card against the terminal.

*Beep.*

The tiny green bulb illuminated. They entered.

The interior was luxurious and modern, with shiny wood-paneled walls and plush leather seating. There were multiple TVs on the walls, as well as a mini fridge and microwave. In the back was a row of lockers. That's where Zack headed, stomping off into the darkness.

"Zack, wait!" she said as she followed.

Zack stopped in the small hallway in the back and looked over the lockers until he found the right one—the one labeled *BROM JENKINS.*

"Wait," Chelsi said again. "I ... I don't know about this. Brom has been loyal to me, and..." She trailed off. "The idea of him betraying me..." She looked at Brom's locker. "I don't know if I can go through with this."

Zack just stared at her. When she was finished, there was a moment as he waited for more. Then he said, "Light."

Again, it took Chelsi a sec to decipher his meaning. She found the light switch, flipped it on. A single overhead light illuminated.

And Zack brought his attention back to the locker. Chelsi looked as well.

"It's locked anyway," she said. "It is a *locker*, after all. I'm not sure what you're expecting to—"

*Whack!*

Zack brought his foot to waist level and kicked outward into the wall of lockers, right by Brom's door. The padlocks rattled, and the edge of Brom's locker buckled. In another swift move, Zack jammed his hands in the newly formed gap in the metal and yanked. With an awful screech, the door tore from its hinges.

Chelsi's mouth hung open.

The entire act had taken but a second. But there had been so much movement in it, so much violence.

Zack looked at her and grinned. He rapped a knuckle on the lockers.

"Flimsy," he said and swallowed.

Chelsi shrugged. "I don't think the bus-maker ever truly had break-ins in mind when they shopped for lockers."

She sighed. And with that, she suddenly felt overwhelmed. A few moments earlier, she had concluded that Zack was some sort of spy. Now, that notion was further solidified, and it was almost too much to handle.

Zack began going through the contents in Brom's locker, tossing them on the floor—toothbrush, toothpaste, umbrella, a leather satchel. He pulled out a binder, flipped through it.

His eyes stopped reading abruptly. He held the binder out for Chelsi to examine—an address was scrawled on one of the documents.

"Hattiesburg," he said and swallowed.

Chelsi gasped at the sound of her hometown.

"*Hattiesburg?*" she said and took the binder from him.

When she saw the address, her heart beat even faster.

"What is it?" Zack said, concern registering through his gravelly voice.

Chelsi had to reach out to the wall to stabilize herself. She tried to speak. Couldn't.

"What is it?" Zack repeated. He swallowed. "Your family? Friends?"

Chelsi shook her head. "No. Neither." She stared at the address for a long moment before she could look back up at Zack. "It's Egly's address."

"Egly?"

Chelsi nodded. "Egly's also from Hattiesburg."

"You knew him..." Zack said and swallowed. "From home?"

She tore her eyes away from the address and looked up at him. She shook her head.

"No, like I told you, he was just a random roadie. One who had an obsession with me. It was a sheer coincidence that he was from Hattiesburg."

"Small world," Zack said with almost a hint of incredulity in his gravelly voice.

She stared back at him for a moment. Then looked at the address again. Then back at Zack.

"So what can this mean that Egly's address was in Brom's locker?" she said.

"It means I'm right," Zack said and swallowed. "Brom is the mole."

Chelsi couldn't believe it. She had trusted Brom for over two years, and he had always been there to protect her. Strong. Broad. Noble. Loyal. And now, without warning, he had betrayed her. The thought of it made her stomach turn.

She looked up at Zack with tears in her eyes, "I can't believe he would do this to me... after everything we've been through together... how could he?"

She shook her head in disbelief as she tried to make sense of it all.

"I guess I should have seen it coming, huh? I'm so damn naïve. But I never imagined..."

Her voice trailed off as she fought back the tears.

Zack said nothing, only bowed his head respectfully, but there was sympathy in his dark eyes.

He pointed a finger at the note.

"It also means..." Another swallow. "We're going to Hattiesburg."

"What?" Chelsi said. "I have to be back on stage in..." She checked her watch. "Shit! Five minutes!"

"Finish concert," Zack said and swallowed. "Then we leave..." Another swallow. "*Alone*."

"I can't just leave my tour! I have the Fourth of July concert tomorrow in Nashville!"

Zack's expression didn't waver.

"I'll get you to Nashville..." He swallowed. "On time."

"And where exactly are we going to stay?" she said, losing patience. "My people will be looking for me. I can't just take this face into any ol' Motel 6."

She gestured with her hand to her facial area, where another red curl had escaped her hoodie.

"I have place we can crash..." Zack said and swallowed. "Midway."

Chelsi couldn't respond, overwhelmed by the moment.

Zack looked past her toward the door where they entered.

"Must get you..." He swallowed. "To your concert."

He flipped off the light switch and stomped away through the darkness toward the door.

Reluctantly, Chelsi followed.

# CHAPTER TWENTY-TWO

CONNOR TOOK a long drag from his cigarette, the smoke swirling around him in the back of the green room. His eyes flicked to the *NO SMOKING* sign on the opposite side of the space, its red letters stark against the white background.

Whatever. He didn't give a shit anymore.

He was leaning against one of the sofas in the back, hiding away from the bright lights of the wall of mirrors, his ass on the armrest. He rubbed his left temple with his free hand as his thoughts darted in a million directions at once.

It had seemed so perfect. Connor had worked damn hard to gain the upper hand in the power struggle of his sister's inner circle, but now everything was slipping out of his grasp. For the last few days, each new development only increased Connor's anxiety, leaving him unsettled and unsure of what the future held.

Now, with the mysterious Zack around, everything was amplified.

He took another long drag.

When he finally brought the cigarette away from his lips, he glanced at his watch.

It had been over an hour and a half. Nearly an hour and forty-five minutes, actually.

Usually, it took her less than one hour.

Of course, Chelsi was surely rattled, what with a rifle being found at the disturbance and then having Big O more or less force her to continue with the concert.

But still...

Connor's mind flashed on Zack again for some reason.

Another drag from the cigarette.

He'd left the door cracked open, and the hinges squeaked as it slowly opened.

Finally!

Though he felt some of the tension slip from the folds of his brow, Connor's immediate relief was quickly neutralized.

Because a single person entered the room. It was neither his sister nor Brom nor Octavius Osgood.

It was one of the security personnel. Connor didn't know his name.

"What is it?" Connor barked at the man.

The man was huge and muscular, but he flinched under Connor's intense gaze. "She's... gone."

A long pause from Connor.

"Who's gone?"

The security guard shifted nervously and replied, "Your sister."

Connor's fingers tightened around the cigarette as he smashed it out on the glass table before him. He hopped to his feet and rushed toward the guard, who looked more intimidated than ever. "*What?*"

"She never came out of the shower facility," the guard said. "It was taking her a lot longer than usual. Didn't respond to our calls. So we had to track down a female guard. When she went in, the facility was empty. She ... vanished."

"Vanished?"

"We've been searching the entire facility for twenty minutes. The Geissler staff, too. And the cops. So we—"

Connor tore his radio off his belt, shoved it in the man's direction. "Why the hell hasn't Brom called me yet?"

Any security matters went straight from Brom to Connor. Always.

"Well, that's why I'm here, sir," the guard said, his eyes going to the floor. "No one can find Brom, either."

"*What?*"

Connor had just asked a question but didn't have time to wait for a response. He didn't have time for *any* of this shit.

He stormed past the guard, across the green room, and into the bright hallway. His hurried footsteps tapped on the polished floor.

Ahead were several more of the security team. All looking in Connor's direction. A couple of them stepped toward him, mouths already forming urgent words.

"Shut up!" Connor said as he breezed past them. He held his radio overhead and shouted, "Just connect me to the damn cops."

Thoughts raced through his mind as he contemplated the possible scenarios and their implications. He had to gain control of the situation. It was a damn good thing he'd been taking proactive measures lately, positioning himself strategically within Chelsi's world.

As he stalked down the hallway, his thoughts focused on the next steps.

# CHAPTER TWENTY-THREE

*Pensacola, Florida*

"Your voice sure does sound familiar, Chelsi," the old woman said. "Are you sure I've never met you before?"

Chelsi glanced at Zack, seated beside Rita Enfield on the porch swing. He shrugged.

"I just have one of those voices, ma'am," Chelsi said.

Mrs. Enfield was a tiny African American woman with blazing white hair and eyes, wearing a floral dress with lace around the edges. Her legs dangled off the porch swing, too short to reach the floor.

The woman's milky eyes scanned over Chelsi as her lips pursed tighter, deepening their wrinkles, not entirely convinced by Chelsi's response. Zack had said his neighbor was completely blind and that she posed no threat of recognizing Chelsi's famous face, but it certainly seemed like Mrs. Enfield was giving Chelsi a visual inspection.

Mrs. Enfield's house was on a quiet street in a sprawling and eclectic neighborhood called East Hill—Victorian homes and ultra-modern ones and everything in between; palm trees and oaks and pines.

Chelsi turned her attention away from Mrs. Enfield and looked out beyond the porch. A couple strolled past with their dog. Through the warm glow of the window across the street, Chelsi saw a happy family enjoying a night of television. The air was soft and fragrant with the scent of Mrs. Enfield's garden and that of nearby magnolias. Chelsi took a deep breath, savoring this fleeting moment of peace.

A strand of hair poked loose. With a quick tug of the sweatshirt's cords, she tightened the hood that covered her head, ensuring her wild curls were fully clamped down. She was doing her best to conceal her famous visage from any prying eyes that might peer onto the darkened porch.

Zack had told her he'd initially driven from Pensacola to Jacksonville. But when he whisked her here, to the opposite end of the Panhandle, he'd quickly arranged a private Learjet. When they landed, a brand-new BMW coupe awaited them at Pensacola International. Chelsi wondered what would become of the vehicle Zack had driven to Jacksonville, but she hadn't asked. One thing was clear: Zack's organization had resources.

Chelsi had never been to Pensacola, Florida, much less the East Hill neighborhood. So when they arrived, she'd asked Zack if he wouldn't mind driving her past a local point of interest—a Pensacola landmark of some sort, something Chelsi could view from the car without risk of drawing attention. She'd needed something—*anything*—to distract herself from the uncertainty ahead.

Instead of showing her a landmark, Zack had taken Chelsi's simple request and exploded it, giving her a full, citywide driving tour in the BMW. A bit of excitement had shown through his stony exterior; he clearly loved his town. His annotations were brief—given that terrible voice of his—but the gesture was ridiculously sweet.

As she studied Zack now on the other side of the porch, Zack glanced at his watch and turned to the tiny woman beside him.

"It's late," he said and swallowed. "Past your bedtime."

Mrs. Enfield smiled. "Oh, I'm too excited to sleep, Si."

"Why?"

"Miss Maven's coming here tomorrow."

Zack's eyes widened. "She wasn't supposed to come..." He swallowed. "Until end of month."

Mrs. Enfield shrugged. "Plans change, dear."

Zack's expression grew more flustered. "We were supposed..." he said and swallowed. "To talk about this."

Mrs. Enfield shook her head. "No, Si, *you* said we'd talk about it. I never agreed to that."

Zack's frustration was palpable now. He looked at Chelsi, then back to Mrs. Enfield. After a few awkward moments, he stood up.

"I don't like this," he said and swallowed. "But you need your sleep."

With that, Zack gently placed a hand on Mrs. Enfield's shoulder and helped her off the porch swing.

Mrs. Enfield brought her lifeless eyes in Chelsi's direction. "Lovely meeting you. Goodnight, dear."

"You too, ma'am," Chelsi said with a smile. "Goodnight, Mrs. Enfield."

Chelsi watched as Zack guided Mrs. Enfield toward the front door. One massive man, one tiny woman. Beauty and the Beast. He handled her with the utmost care, like she was made of porcelain.

The charm of the moment stirred something inside Chelsi's mind—that special, cordoned-off part of her mind reserved solely for her art. Lyrics fell into place.

Zack shut the door behind Mrs. Enfield. He looked at Chelsi and motioned for her to follow as he stepped off the porch.

————

Chelsi wondered why Zack—whose organization was clearly loaded—lived in such a simple place. From the outside, his house looked like a modest mid-century home, maybe two-bedroom, humble and somewhat plain. Puzzling.

But when she stepped inside and Zack flipped on the lights, a sense of discordance quickly erased some of the mystery. The place was like something straight out of an L.A. design magazine—all blacks and whites and silvers and grays with streaks of glass and brushed metals. Oversized plants were placed here and there, as were a few abstract-design accent pieces.

"If it's not too prying," Chelsi said as Zack shut and locked the door behind them, "may I ask you something? You seemed awfully concerned about Miss Maven visiting Mrs. Enfield. Who's Miss Maven?"

"A con artist bitch," Zack said without looking at her as he stepped past, going to the kitchen.

Well, now...

Only moments earlier, Chelsi had thought Zack must have been a softie on the inside—with his thoughtful tour of Pensacola and the tenderness with which he'd treated his elderly neighbor.

Now Chelsi saw the wolf again.

"She kept calling you 'Si,'" Chelsi said. "That some sort of nickname?"

"Yes."

Zack opened the black refrigerator, revealing a nearly empty interior—just a few condiments on the door and a six-pack of Heineken on the center shelf. He grabbed one of the bottles, turned in Chelsi's direction, and lifted both the beer and his eyebrows in a gesture that said, *Want one?*

Chelsi shook her head. "No, thanks."

Zack grabbed a bottle opener from a nearby drawer, popped the cap, took a swig, and then pointed at the sectional sofa dominating the opposite side of the open floor plan.

"Me," he said. He turned the finger so that it was pointing to the small hallway at the back of the house. "You."

She saw a bathroom door, open, and a pair of bedroom doors, both cracked. The smaller bedroom was bathed in an eerie blue light, and the source was immediately apparent—a sensory deprivation pod. The curved gap between its top and base looked like a grin, leering at Chelsi, artificial blue light pouring out. The pod's footprint filled the entire room.

What an odd thing for a person to have in one's home, particularly a house on the smaller side. The pod must've cost a fortune. Once more, she was reminded of how much money Zack and his organization seemed to have.

And again, she recognized what a peculiar individual Zack was...

Regardless, Zack was clearly indicating not the sensory-deprivation chamber but the other room, where Chelsi could see the corner of a bed with a dark comforter. Zack meant for her to sleep in the bed while he would sleep on the sectional.

Chelsi looked back at him. "It's been a long day, and you've done a lot for me. You don't need to sleep on the couch. We could sleep together."

She flushed. Her hands went to her mouth.

"Wait!" she said and stepped toward him. "I didn't mean *sleep* together; I meant *sleep* together. Like, you know, in the same bed."

Zack looked at her. Blinked. And without a word, he

stepped away, going to a nearby closet where he retrieved blankets and pillows for his evening on the sofa. Chelsi watched.

"All right, Zack," she said softly. "Goodnight, then."

Zack grunted and flashed her a quick nod as he busied himself with his makeshift bed preparation.

She stepped past him to the back bedroom, turned on the nightstand lamp, and closed the door behind her. The design of the main living area carried into the bedroom—black-and-white furniture, a California king adorned with all-black bedding, and a spirally metal art piece that reminded Chelsi a bit of her own hair. There was also a desk with a computer and a fax machine on a small table in the corner.

She dropped onto the edge of the mattress and allowed herself a moment of vulnerability, acknowledging the fear that nagged at the edges of her consciousness. A long sigh. Then forced herself past self-pity. She turned off the lamp.

Darkness. Insects chirped outside, just beyond the window.

As she slipped beneath the black sheets, Zack's bed enveloped her. Thoughts of Zack and their shared journey echoed in her mind, forcing out the concerns and uncertainties that clouded her thoughts.

She closed her eyes.

# CHAPTER TWENTY-FOUR

*Hattiesburg, Mississippi*

THE MORNING SKY hung heavy with gray, brooding clouds, casting an eerie pallor over the destitute neighborhood. Silence parked the BMW on a patch of crumbling asphalt. Wretched houses with broken windows loomed on all sides.

It had taken a little over two and a half hours to get there from Pensacola. They'd left before the sun rose. Silence's brand-new car had received a true trial by fire and passed with flying colors, proving to be an excellent highway driver. It had twenty-two miles on the odometer when they departed; it now had 177.

Two blocks back, Silence had caught another glimpse of the blue Lincoln. He'd caught two previous glimpses of it in the sprawling neighborhood since exiting off Highway 98. When the Lincoln turned, he'd seen that it bore an Ohio plate. The man behind the wheel was hefty.

And his silhouette looked familiar.

Perhaps Silence was being paranoid, but he filed the notion away in his chaotic brain space nonetheless. In his line of work, the boundary between *paranoid* and *prudent* was frequently assaulted.

Silence and Chelsi stepped out of the car, their footsteps muffled by the overgrown weeds clawing their way through the cracks in the pavement. Chelsi wore the sweatshirt again, keeping all that hair out of sight. Silence had asked her to stay in the vehicle, and she had vehemently substantiated the stereotype of a fiery redhead. So there she was beside him.

Ahead of them, the house's timeworn structure sagged under the weight of despair. Peeling paint revealed the decaying wood beneath. Shattered glass glinted in the grass.

"My God," Chelsi said. "I mean, it wasn't exactly a nice place two years ago, but I can't believe it got *this* bad so quickly."

Silence turned to her. "You went..." he said and swallowed. "To a roadie's house?"

Chelsi nodded. "Team-building stuff, sure."

Hmm...

Silence stored another nagging notion away in the file cabinets of his torrential mind, right beside his fresh note about the blue Lincoln from Ohio.

As they crunched up the pair of steps in front of the door, Chelsi hesitated, her voice laced with uncertainty. "Should we really be here, Zack?"

Silence didn't respond, his gaze fixed on the door. A breeze whispered through the desolation. He lifted a hand to knock, and—

His cellular phone vibrated in his pocket.

He would typically ignore it at a moment like this. But not this time. There was a call he was desperately anticipating.

He pulled the phone from his pocket. The LCD screen on the front showed the call was from the Watchers.

*Yes!*

He flipped it open. "A-23."

A Specialist responded. Male voice with a smoker's rasp. "It's a website. There are plenty of 'Nexuses' out there, but ours is a location on the World Wide Web."

"What kind..." Silence said and swallowed. "Of website?"

"Our investigation isn't complete," the Specialist said with a peculiar undercurrent of snark. "And you're in the field."

"But—"

It was too late.

*Beep*.

Shit!

Silence growled, staring at *CALL ENDED* on his cellular. A moment of this, then he collapsed the phone and returned it to his pocket.

Chelsi looked at him quizzically.

"Long story," Silence said and pointed to the BMW. "Go back to car."

"No."

Ugh.

Silence looked away from her and returned to what he was doing before the phone call. He knocked.

They waited.

Quiet in the neighborhood surrounding them. More whistling breeze. A dog barking. Somewhere, a man laughed. It sounded wicked.

No reply.

Silence knocked again.

More waiting.

Then they heard something from inside.

But not a reply.

*It was a scream*.

An anguished, blood-curdling bellow from somewhere in the bowels of the house.

Silence and Chelsi exchanged a look, then Silence shoved

her backward and to the side, beyond the doorframe.

"Don't follow!" he shouted, a shot of pain burning his throat.

His hand went to the holster at his side, fingers wrapping around the cold grip of his Beretta.

"*What are you doing?*" Chelsi said.

With one swift motion, Silence kicked the door. The splintered wood groaned as the door flew inside. It had put up little resistance.

Silence cleared the doorway, sweeping left, right.

The interior of the house mirrored the desolation of its exterior. Dust particles danced in the dim light that filtered through the tattered curtains, which cast elongated shadows. Rotted furniture lay scattered across the floor. An out-of-place laptop computer was on a card desk at the far wall.

Silence narrowed his eyes as he moved inside. The muffled screams grew louder. It was a man.

Someone was being tortured. Or he was dying. Or both.

Following the anguished cries, Silence navigated the dilapidation, his movements a blur of purpose. The wails intensified, reverberating off the walls.

The hallway. The screams were coming from the hallway ahead.

He followed the sound until it led him to a closed bathroom door at the back of the house. The shrieks were piercingly loud now, right on the other side of the door.

The smell was worse, too. Now it was more than just mold. Silence smelled feces.

He wrapped his hand around the doorknob. Locked.

With a surge of adrenaline, Silence kicked the door like he had the other one a few moments prior. Decayed wood shards flew all around him, peppering his arms, legs, face.

And the grotesque sight made him instinctively turn his head.

# CHAPTER TWENTY-FIVE

LENNY'S HEART thundered as he pulled his Lincoln up a block away from the dilapidated house. He understood from his encyclopedic knowledge of Chelsi Nichols trivia—coupled with his prodigious Internet skills—that the house belonged to one of her roadies, a guy who left her inner circle two years ago. Though Lenny had trekked to Hattiesburg multiple times since he began his full-on obsession with Chelsi a couple of years ago, he'd never really felt creepy about it.

This time, even he had to admit it was kind of weird to be outside the home of a former staff member of Chelsi's.

But that wasn't what was making his heart pound in his chest—it was a pair of other notions. First, there she was! Chelsi Mae herself. Standing outside the crappy house. She wore a hooded sweatshirt to hide her famous curls, but Lenny would recognize her under full camouflage in a thick jungle; he would recognize her anywhere.

She was only yards away from him. He'd been this close to her before. Closer, even. Many times. But in those instances, she'd been on a stage, she'd been performing, she'd been covered in thick makeup and garish outfits.

Now, she was before him in the real world. Wearing a simple gray sweatshirt.

On any normal day, that would be the main reason his heart was thundering. But if he was being truthful, it was the other factor that was really making his heart pound—a man's horrendous screaming coming from the open doorway of the rundown house.

Lenny watched as Chelsi shifted nervously from foot to foot, her hands clasped together tightly, her face darting back and forth. She was clearly apprehensive at the awful sound emitting from the space right before her, but she neither entered the house nor sprinted away from it. She just stayed rooted in place.

What the hell was going on over there?

Just then, a trio of musclebound men—who looked too clean-cut to belong to this terrible neighborhood in their fresh-looking T-shirts and jeans—exited the rear of the property and circled around from the west side of the house...

...heading toward Chelsi.

Lenny's heart thundered harder yet as he witnessed the unfolding danger. His mouth went dry as he realized there was no way he could get to her before they did.

Or could he?

Was he frozen in place with cowardice?

Suddenly, the three men stopped before rounding the corner of the house. They converged, heads lowered toward each other, clearly discussing their plan in hushed tones.

Lenny quaked, his body trembling as he attempted to summon the courage to interfere. His throat grew tight, and his mind spun in circles, tormenting him with different scenarios of what could happen if he stepped forward...

...or if he didn't.

# CHAPTER TWENTY-SIX

SILENCE BURST into the decrepit bathroom, forcing his face to a forward orientation after its involuntary sideways recoil. In a fraction of a second, he cleared the room with swift precision, then his trained eyes scanned every corner.

Broken mirror. Overturned toilet. Litter-strewn floor. Countertop with a tape recorder and a rotary telephone.

Then Silence's gaze returned to the clawfoot tub, to the chilling sight he'd first glimpsed when the door flew open after he'd kicked it in.

Brom Jenkins.

Slaughtered.

Absolutely hacked to pieces.

The immediate realization that Brom *wasn't* a traitor—rather, that the man was bait—was instantly erased by a knot of rage coiling in Silence's chest. His mind flashed on Egly, that sneering face he'd seen on the other side of the fence in Jacksonville.

The lifeless body was slumped over the rim of the tub. Brom's face was tilted to the side, the only part of him that wasn't sliced up. An intentional omission, no doubt. Deep gashes crisscrossed Brom's mutilated form. His limbs were hacked and mangled. Jagged edges of torn sinew. Flesh hung in long strips.

There was no water in the tub. No need. Brom was taking a bath in his own blood. The copper scent of it filled the air.

Brom was very much dead. And it looked like he had been for a while.

Yet the unsettling screams persisted.

Silence turned his attention to the tape recorder on the countertop—the source of the noise.

A realization washed over Silence, cutting through the haze of shock.

He'd been set up.

The grisly scene, the screams on the tape recorder—it was all part of a meticulously crafted trap.

His instincts instantly kicked into overdrive as he whipped around to the door he had kicked open moments earlier...

Only to see it slamming shut with a metallic clang.

He bounded toward the door, grabbed the handle. Locked.

He looked up. A stainless steel pneumatic shaft with an arm—like an oversized door closer—was at the top edge of the door.

His gaze shifted to the right and found a tiny camera mounted in the upper right-hand corner of the room. A red bulb was alight.

Silence reared back and drove his shoulder into the door.

*Bang!*

Sharp pain surged through him as an odd sound emitted from the seemingly rotten wood.

*Seemingly* rotten.

It was steel-reinforced.

He'd thought it felt odd when he kicked it. Egly must

have released the door's hold from a distance just before Silence kicked it. There must have been tiny cameras all over the shithole house.

The room was windowless.

He was locked in. Trapped.

Silence's newest revelation was sicker even than the others: Egly had captured him.

It was then he heard Chelsi scream from the front of the house.

# CHAPTER TWENTY-SEVEN

LENNY HAD FINALLY WORKED up the nerve to leave his Lincoln, to bolt over to the house.

But it was too late.

He could almost see the future unfolding before him. Everything moved in slow-motion, yet he had to act fast. His legs powered forward towards the menacing figures closing on Chelsi. He screamed at them, and his cry seemed to snag on the still air, getting sucked up and lost to nothingness before it even had a chance to get to her.

The men, if they even registered the sound, were undeterred. With a sudden burst of speed, they all three converged on Chelsi. She screamed again.

The first man came at her with a wild swipe of the arms, trying to wrap Chelsi up. Chelsi ducked quickly and used the momentum of her movement to drive forward and slam the man in the chest with all her might. He staggered back, stunned by the impact of her attack. The other two men hesitated just long enough for Chelsi to spin around, but the punch she swung was swallowed up by one of the brute's massive hands while the other two wrapped her up, lifting her off the ground as she kicked and thrashed. Her hood flew off, and all of those red curls sprang out.

Suddenly, there was a screech of tires, and a panel van burst into view, swerving around the corner. The side door slammed open, and Lenny watched in horror as two more men leaped out of the van, joining the other three and bundling Chelsi quickly and efficiently into the back of the vehicle.

The van hardly even slowed. The driver hit the accelerator, and within seconds, the van was gone, its tires screaming. Lenny skidded to a stop, panting heavily, his heart sinking in despair.

He'd been too late.

He'd hesitated too long.

No matter how hard he had tried, he hadn't been able to reach Chelsi in time. Now she was a captive of some unknown force.

Lenny had failed. Maybe everyone back in Lima was right about him after all.

Guilt gnawed at him as he considered what might be happening to Chelsi Nichols right then, and a sense of helplessness washed over his entire being. He had no idea who the mysterious men were or where they had taken Chelsi, let alone how to extricate her.

He shook his head and straightened up in an effort to regain some semblance of dignity. Giving into despair wouldn't help the situation; instead, he needed to think clearly and take action.

But what action?

Lenny's gaze drifted over the street before him, looking for any sign of the van that had bolted away with Chelsi, but there was nothing—no clue as to its destination or identity. Lenny had to return empty-handed yet again.

He was about to turn away in dejection when suddenly, a

series of loud bangs pierced the morning air. He whipped around, his heart racing.

*Bam! Bam! Bam!*

The sound reverberated through the desolation of the street. It sounded like someone pounding on a wall, desperate to escape.

It was coming from...

The house.

The house to Lenny's right, past the sidewalk on which he stood. The house from which Chelsi was just abducted.

Hesitation warred within Lenny again. Unlike last time, though, there was no sense of duty to contend with. In fact, logic was telling him to do just the opposite of something honorable; it was telling him he should flee. At best, he should find help, perhaps contact the authorities.

Yet something was calling him toward the source of the noise.

He moved.

Lenny steeled himself as he marched towards the yawning entrance of the house. His legs quaked, but his feet kept going. With each step closer, he inhaled more deeply, trying steady the rumbling in his stomach.

And all the while, the banging continued.

*Bam! Bam! Bam!*

# CHAPTER TWENTY-EIGHT

SILENCE'S massive shoulder collided with the steel-reinforced door. His relentless pounding reverberated through the bathroom with each futile impact.

But as Silence paused for a moment, sweat dripping down his forehead, he glanced at the door again. His eyes traced the powerful pneumatics at the top of the door, then headed south, examining the steel bars running vertically over its length, clearly visible through the rotten wood. It was a castle gate impervious to Silence's brute strength.

*Ring!*

Silence whipped around.

The phone. On the counter. Inches from the tape recorder, still emitting the horrible screams.

The damn phone was ringing.

*Ring!*

Without hesitation, Silence reached for it. He knew exactly who was on the other end of the line.

Silence raised the receiver to his ear.

"Ah, Zack," said a melodic yet off-kilter voice. "I trust you've figured it out by now."

Silence cringed at Egly's contented tone.

"Yes," he muttered as he pressed *STOP* on the tape recorder. The screaming ceased, and in the noise's absence, Silence now heard police sirens in the distance.

Silence had indeed figured it out. His turbulent mind had been working in the background while his body tried desperately to bust through an impenetrable door. He had a pretty damn good idea of how Egly had trapped him.

"You must've thought Brom was an inside man," Egly said. "The person on Chelsi's security team who got me the key to the tower, who supplied the rifle. So you went to his locker, found the Hattiesburg address. *My* Hattiesburg address. By then, you knew you had your man. Turns out, Brom was just as valiant and devoted as he acted. He wasn't a true warrior, though. When push came to shove, he whined like a bitch. Those were genuine screams on the audiotape. Brom's. Played on a loop."

Silence glanced at the tape recorder. He gritted his teeth.

"So we set up a nice long trail of clues that led you right there to the trap." Egly paused. And in a cartoonish voice, he added, "And you fell for it, mister."

A single word Egly said stuck out in Silence's mind, blazing like a spotlight.

"Who's 'we'?" Silence said.

"The door only opens from the outside," Egly said, ignoring his question.

Silence's eyes returned to the door and scanned the pneumatics.

"The doorknob is fixed so that it feels locked," Egly continued. "But you could have pushed it open with your pinky finger. You didn't have to kick it so hard!"

Egly laughed.

"I probably don't need to tell you this, but the police will be there soon," he said. "They've been told the murderer almost got away, but an anonymous good Samaritan managed to lock him in the bathroom with the victim."

Silence slowly turned and looked at the destroyed body in the tub behind him.

Outside, the sirens were a bit louder, a bit nearer.

Silence swallowed. "What—"

But before he could finish, there was a rattle on the line. Egly had hung up.

Silence slammed the receiver down.

The sound of approaching sirens intensified. Sweat flushed Silence's skin, over his entire body. His mind raced, tumbling into mental oblivion, and C.C.'s voice came to him.

*Calm, love. Calm.*

This time, he couldn't take her advice. He could hardly even hear her.

Thoughts swirled in his mind.

The sirens.

He looked back. Blood. So much blood.

Which brought a quick flash of a memory.

*C.C. murdered.*

*So much of her blood.*

*Lying on the hardwood floor in a puddle of her blood.*

Sirens.

Those damn sirens.

Yet, as the cacophony outside reached its crescendo, a new noise pierced the chaos—a set of footsteps on the other side of the door.

# CHAPTER TWENTY-NINE

LENNY STOOD outside the bathroom door, his heart pounding in his chest. The distant sound of sirens filled the air.

Again, his inner voice screamed at him.

*What the hell are you doing here?*

Moments earlier, as he stood at the open doorway outside, the banging sound he'd heard abruptly halted. Then there had been the ringing of a telephone. Then the screaming stopped. Then he heard a wicked-sounding, gravelly voice holding an urgent phone conversation.

Yet that strange impulse of his had *still* compelled him to cross the threshold and move through the home—a place of cracked walls and moldy floors—all the way to a closed bathroom door. The crackling voice had come from inside the bathroom.

"Who's there?" the voice called from behind the door.

Lenny jumped. The ruinous sound of the voice was alarming.

"Um ... my name's Lenny. I ... I just saw Chelsi Nichols get abducted outside, and—"

"*What?* Shit!"

"You're part of her security, aren't you?" Lenny said.

A slight pause. "Yes. Zack."

"Was that you I saw in Jacksonville last night?" Lenny said. "The man who chased off after Malcolm Egly?"

"Yes. Egly locked me in here with..." There was a pause. "Someone he murdered." Another pause. "Need you to let me out."

"How would I do that?"

"Door opens..." A pause. "From your side only."

Lenny looked down at the doorknob, tried it. Locked. He placed his hand on the door, applied a small amount of pressure. It was surprisingly heavy, but he could feel it move.

The sirens were louder. Must've been within blocks now.

"Hurry!" Zack said.

"How can I trust you? How do I know you are who you say you are?"

Another momentary pause, and then a plastic card slid under the door. Lenny picked it up. He recognized it—one of Chelsi's security staff IDs. It bore her logo—the elaborate font paired with the graphics of nickels and red curls—as well as *SECURITY* and a serial number.

This man *was* one of Chelsi's.

But...

It never hurt to be cautious.

Surveying his surroundings, Lenny's gaze fell upon a rusty curtain rod propped up in the corner. He grabbed it, held it over his head, and with the other hand, he gave the heavy door a shove.

The door swung open, and Lenny saw something that almost made him vomit—the body of Brom Jenkins, Chelsi's head of security, lying in an old-fashioned bathtub, butchered to bloody pieces.

But before Lenny could fully comprehend what he'd seen,

he was grabbed and pulled. In the blink of an eye, Lenny found himself grappling with a beastly opponent—the same hulking man he had seen in Jacksonville. Lenny now knew him as Zack.

Lenny clenched onto the rusty curtain rod, but the other man disarmed him with a swift motion. The rod slipped from Lenny's grasp, clattering to the hardwood.

With a powerful shove, Lenny was sent sprawling onto the floor, his body sliding for a moment before crashing into the wall. Pain radiated through his limbs as he scrambled to right himself, but before he could move, the towering figure loomed above him.

Lenny's senses heightened, every muscle tensed with anticipation. He saw Zack pull back for a strike, and he covered his face.

But no blow came.

Lenny opened his eyes.

Zack had his hand extended.

"Come on!" he said.

The wail of the sirens now filled the house. They must've been within blocks.

Zack yanked Lenny to his feet like he weighed nothing at all, no small task given Lenny's weight wasn't "nothing"; it was 237.

They ran for the front door, and as they did, Zack swerved to the right, to the small desk by the front door that Lenny had spotted when he entered. Without breaking stride, Zack grabbed the plastic file box and laptop computer, yanking the latter's cords straight out of the wall—a power cord and a phone line.

They burst outside. Blue and red lights appeared in the distance out of the dissipating morning haze.

"This way!" Lenny said.

And he ran for the Lincoln with Zack in tow.

# CHAPTER THIRTY

THE SUN HAD JUST RISEN over Egly's hometown of Hattiesburg, casting a red-orange hue on the morning mist hanging over the long-abandoned parking lot, an expanse of cracked pavement overgrown with weeds and long grass. The only sound was the occasional chirp of a passing bird; otherwise, the air was still and silent.

For Egly, who stood at the edge of the lot, it felt like the world had gone into hiding. That was fine by him. Isolation suited him—always had—and it had proven conducive to his mission. He'd been in the parking lot for close to forty-five minutes now, waiting for the van with the hired men and the person they were to have secured.

A tingle of hope arose as he heard a vehicle somewhere ahead. He ran his hands together, stared at the corner...

And there it appeared.

The white panel van, its headlights cutting through the thick morning fog.

With a smile stretching across his face, Egly waited as the van pulled to a stop a few feet in front of him. The side door slid open, and the goons—men provided by Egly's partner—

dragged Chelsi out. She was frazzled, but not nearly as much as one would expect, given her situation. Chelsi was resilient.

God, Egly loved this woman.

Her lip trembled, and her eyes darted around the ruined urban landscape, looking for an escape route. One of the men kept a hand firmly clenched on her arm.

Egly stepped closer, within feet of her, relishing the moment.

"Chelsi," he said, the word coming out almost like a sigh. For a moment, he couldn't find any other words. Then he said, "How have you been?"

Chelsi's eyes widened with a mixture of recognition and dread, a silent acknowledgment of their shared history. Egly savored the power he held over her, the secrets that bound them.

She didn't respond.

He sighed again. "If only this was a perfect world. None of this had to happen."

Chelsi's voice quivered as she spoke, her words laced with a mixture of fear and defiance. "What is this, Malcolm? Why are you doing this?"

"For you," he said, his tone earnest.

"Did you..." She stopped, swallowed. "Did you kill those people, Malcolm?"

Egly stuck his hands in his pockets. "There's so much that won't make sense to you. Not yet. Not until—"

"*Did you kill those people?*"

Egly debated his response. Paused a beat. And nodded.

Chelsi shuddered, and her lip trembled harder. The color drained from her face.

"Each concert since D.C., there's been one kill," Egly said. "Or an attempted kill, anyway. But tonight, your concert tour ends. With a bang! The Fourth of July, baby! Which means—"

Chelsi cut him off. "Y-you're going to do something

terrible in Nashville, aren't you? Something even bigger, even worse."

Egly shrugged and gave her his best *Ain't I a stinker?* look.

Chelsi's voice wavered as she responded, her fear mingled with a glimmer of defiance. "Malcolm, why are you doing this?"

"A blood pact," Egly said. "I messed up in Jacksonville, but there's still a chance in Nashville. I mean, I already have you; you're right in front of me; but I'm not allowed to call you mine until I complete my task."

Chelsi raised an eyebrow. Her lip stopped trembling. She stepped closer to him, fighting against the grip of the hired muscle holding her arm.

"You're 'not allowed'?" she said. "What does that mean?"

Suddenly, Egly realized he'd shared too much.

His smile widened as he motioned at the goons. They took his meaning and dragged Chelsi to Egly's pickup truck, waiting on the other side of the parking lot. Chelsi kicked, thrashed, screamed at them.

And, with his hands still in his pocket, Egly whistled as he followed.

# CHAPTER THIRTY-ONE

Of all places to suddenly end up right in the heat of an investigation, Silence found himself in a luxury hotel room.

Not for sleep.

For a telephone jack.

No other options had presented themselves as a place where he could set up Egly's laptop computer. He hadn't been able to find an Internet cafe. In need of a phone jack and desperate, Silence had simply booked a room at the nearest hotel, which was a five-star affair. Silence had paid two hundred dollars and done so in cash, a standard Watchers practice.

The room was exquisite. Its walls were painted a warm, golden hue, and the high ceiling gave it an airy feel. The furniture was crafted from mahogany and decorated with elaborate carvings and gilded frames.

Silence had quickly set up the laptop on the desk and plugged it into the wall jack. But before delving into Malcolm Egly's digital assets, he needed to learn the identity of the other man sharing the hotel room with him.

So far, Silence only had a name. Lenny Ward. The man

had provided that in the Lincoln. Otherwise, their brief, frantic time spent together since leaving Egly's dilapidated house behind was spent locating the hotel.

Silence approached Ward, looked him over. He did know *one* thing about the guy for sure: this was the man Silence had seen in the trees outside the tour buses in Jacksonville, the man who'd been watching him and Chelsi.

Ward was overweight and unkempt. His ill-fitting clothes hung loosely off his body, including the T-shirt bearing Chelsi's face. He had a pale complexion, and both his hair and beard were white-and-gray. The bags under his slightly sunken, sad eyes told a story of weariness.

Silence wouldn't use the label in the real world, but if there was ever someone who fit the moniker of "fat slob," it was this guy.

And if Silence was being honest with himself, he was put off by the notion that this middle-aged guy with a gray beard was apparently a devoted fan of a young, vibrant country music star. It seemed a bit pathetic.

"Saw you in Jax," Silence said and swallowed. "How did you know where to find..." Another swallow. "Chelsi here in Hattiesburg?"

"Because I'm a fan, man," Ward said, pointing at his sweat-stained T-shirt. The cadence of his words had been desperate and fast for no apparent reason. "I'm the perennial loser. At least that's what my family and friends tell me, even though I have money—a good investment after working my ass off on my business for ten years. Maybe they're right about me ... I don't know."

He paused, searching Silence for affirmation.

Well, that would explain why the guy hadn't seemed impressed by the luxurious hotel room. Ward had money, even if his clothing didn't show it.

"That doesn't explain..." Silence said and swallowed. "How you got here." Another swallow. "Talk."

With hands trembling with a mix of excitement and nervousness, Lenny reached into his satchel. He retrieved a gaudy, teeny-bopper promotional magazine adorned with Chelsi's radiant smile on the cover. The glossy pages were splashed with vibrant colors, glittering text, and candid snapshots of the idol, capturing the exuberance of her ardent fan base.

As Lenny flipped through the magazine, each page seemed to pulsate with the infectious energy of Chelsi's music career. His fingertips halted on a particular spread featuring a photo of Chelsi surrounded by her dedicated crew, standing against the backdrop of a luxurious tour bus. The caption said *ROADIES MAKE ROAD TRIPS FUN.*

Silence's eyes narrowed. There, among the roadies, was Egly, the man Silence had chased at the concert. The man who'd looked Silence in the eye and sneered when he admitted to slaughtering a twelve-year-old child.

"I know all the inside information about Chelsi," Lenny said. "I'm really what you would call a super fan. And I know that Malcolm Egly was more than just a roadie."

Silence arched an eyebrow. "How so?"

"Well, about a year ago—"

Silence's cellular phone rang in his pocket, making both men start.

Anticipating the purpose of the call, Silence anxiously fished the phone out of his pocket, checked the screen, and answered.

"A-23."

A Specialist responded. Female voice. Light and airy and young. But deadly serious.

"Okay, Suppressor, we've finished our investigation, and

though we know you're in the middle of a mission, we also know you're eager to hear what we found."

"Yes," Silence said, trying not to sound *too* eager.

"Nexus is a sham journalist site. Sensationalism. A digital rag. On the surface, it looks like any other wannabe mover-and-shaker site, but we dug deeper into the life of Fred 'Slick' Chambers. Seems he arranges all the scenarios that populate Nexus."

Silence cocked his head. "Huh?"

"Chambers coordinates criminal activity, giving him material for the news stories he writes on Nexus."

Ugh, Slick was an even bigger slimeball than Silence had already believed.

"Thought you'd like to know," the Specialist said.

*Beep.*

The Specialist was gone.

———

A few minutes later, Silence had Egly's laptop up and running.

But he wasn't checking the man's files. He was using his Internet browser.

With the information that the Specialist had just given him, it took no time at all to find Nexus. It had been there the whole time, hidden in plain sight. Sometimes, the most complicated questions come with the simplest answers.

Nexus was just as the Specialist had described— a sensationalistic online news site, a tawdry tabloid given the digital treatment. Flashy graphics. Wild headlines. Bizarre and shocking images. Silence clicked the *ABOUT* link.

And there was Slick.

Fred Chambers.

He was described as an attorney-turned-journalist, a nomad in a luxury vehicle, a man who shot all around the country, offering pro bono work to the "victims" he encountered while digging up his stories.

What it didn't say was that the man was a con artist. Someone who prayed on other people's crimes, their pain.

A con artist, like Miss Maven in Pensacola, taking advantage of a little old blind lady.

But much worse.

Silence exhaled, allowing his bulk to sink back into the luxurious leather desk chair. He thought for a moment. Then looked across the room and saw Ward step out of the bathroom, wiping water from his hands.

Oh, yeah. That's right. The *current* mission.

Shit.

C.C.'s voice came to him. *Focus, love.*

She was right.

Realigning his thoughts, Silence closed the Internet browser and opened Malcolm Egly's hard drive.

# CHAPTER THIRTY-TWO

CHELSI STARED out the window as Egly drove through Hattiesburg, her hometown. It had been over a year since she'd been back, and now that she was, the mood was spoiled with her captivity. She remembered the vibrant shops, the friendly faces of the locals, and the smells of the distinctive restaurants. But now, all those things were clouded in her mind with fear and anxiety.

Egly drove down a favorite street of Chelsi's, passing the old theater—the Holly Morton Theater—where she and Connor used to perform. Chelsi could still hear the cheers and laughter of the crowd, feel the energy of the music vibrating through her, and see the way Connor's face lit up when the audience sang along to their songs.

In her mind, Chelsi was transported back to that magical night, the first time she took the spotlight at the age of ten, with her fiery red hair cascading down her shoulders. The theater was filled with an excited buzz as the audience settled into their seats, anticipation hanging in the air like a sweet melody.

The stage was adorned with vibrant lights, casting

colorful hues on their faces. Connor, just eight years old, stood beside her, clutching his miniature guitar, eyes shining with pride and excitement. No one yet had a clue that Chelsi would become a star, so at that time, Connor was her partner in a shared musical journey, providing background vocals and adding an aww-shucks charm to their performances.

As the curtains lifted, Chelsi felt a surge of nervous energy swirling through her. The soft strumming of the guitar filled the air, and she took a deep breath, ready to share her voice with the city. The first notes resonated, their melody reaching the hearts of the audience.

The spotlight embraced Chelsi, illuminating her in a warm embrace, and she closed her eyes, surrendering herself to the music. The lyrics flowed effortlessly from her lips, carrying the emotions of the songs—old country classics—across the theater. Her voice, pure and powerful, soared through the air, intertwining with Connor's harmonies.

The audience responded with applause and cheers, their faces beaming with admiration. Chelsi could feel the love and support enveloping her, igniting a fire within her soul. Chelsi could tell, even then, that the audience was *genuinely* impressed; they were appreciating a true talent, not just a young talent. The energy in the theater was electric, the connection between performer and audience palpable.

The memories flooded back, as vivid as ever. Chelsi remembered the gentle breeze that flowed through the open windows, carrying the scent of freshly bloomed flowers. She felt the floorboards creaking through the soles of her pink cowboy boots.

She recalled the way Connor's voice paired with hers, their voices blending seamlessly, creating a musical tapestry that resonated with the crowd.

Time seemed to stand still as they performed that night,

and now it was a moment frozen in time, etched forever in Chelsi's heart.

As Egly continued to drive, Chelsi wiped away a tear, a mixture of nostalgia and sorrow. The memory of that special night at the Holly Morton Theater was so very distant now, its warmth and innocence worlds away from the fear and uncertainty she now faced.

Another tear rolled down her cheek.

She was Egly's prisoner, and he was taking her to Nashville. She didn't know what his plan for her was or what wicked deed he intended to commit at the concert. But she had a feeling that whatever it was, it would be much worse than what he'd already done.

Which was a sickening notion.

She turned on him and found him with both hands on the wheel, staring straight ahead at the highway. And smiling broadly. The creep was smiling ear to ear.

"Who is it? Your person on the inside," Chelsi said.

Egly didn't reply, didn't look at her, didn't stop smiling.

"If it wasn't Brom," Chelsi continued. "Then who is it?"

Still nothing from Egly.

"Answer me!"

Egly didn't look at her, and he didn't stop smiling, but this time he replied. "Not tellin'. But I will say this—after your friend Zack looks at the materials I left behind in the house, he's going to think *you're* my accomplice, that we planned this out together."

He laughed.

Chelsi immediately understood what "materials" Egly had referred to. He had taken photographs—*multiple* photographs —of the two of them during their two excursions. It was sad. Pathetic in the truest sense.

But since Chelsi had obliged him so openly—with her

trademark smile as bright as ever—those photos had to appear, on first glance, like pictures of a happy couple.

Egly was right. Zack would take one look at the photographs and think she was Egly's accomplice.

As for Chelsi, her suspicion flashed to Connor.

Her brother.

If she was being truthful with herself, she'd suspected him somewhere deep in her subconscious for a long time, even more so than Brom.

But then Chelsi thought back to her moments-earlier set of memories.

At the Holly Morton Theater.

For a long time, Chelsi had found herself grappling with conflicting emotions about Connor. There were moments when she questioned his motives, his seemingly aggressive pursuit of power within her inner circle, and the clashes he had with Octavius Osgood. Connor's behavior could be interpreted as controlling, attempting to shape her career according to his own vision, despite the fact that *she* was the star.

At times, it seemed as if Connor's ambition had taken a sinister turn. His relentless drive to assert himself in Chelsi's life had fueled doubts and suspicions in her mind. She had almost succumbed to the notion that he could be in cahoots with Egly.

But then, like that gentle breeze that had drifted across the Holly Morton stage, Chelsi's recent memories flooded through her mind once more. The sound of Chelsi and Connor, on that stage, their harmonious voices blending in perfect synchronization, shattered the doubts that had briefly clouded her judgment.

He was her brother.

Egly had taken so much from her. But he wasn't going to taint her memories of childhood with Connor. He wasn't going to make her suspect her own brother, no matter how power-hungry, jealous, and even mean he had turned.

No matter how it appeared from the outside, Chelsi knew deep within her heart that Connor's actions were not driven by evil intent. His ambition, his passionate pursuit of influence within her inner circle, stemmed from a place of genuine concern and a desire to protect her. He saw her talent, her potential, and wanted to guide her towards a path that he believed would lead to even greater success.

*He was her brother.*

She would put her faith in that, not on seemingly damning exterior appearances.

The truck came to a stop at a red light, and Chelsi took a deep breath. She had to stay strong, be brave. If she didn't, she had no idea what Egly would do. He'd already proven himself to be a violent and unpredictable man.

The truck moved again, and Chelsi watched as the landscape of Hattiesburg disappeared from view. She was leaving the place that was once her home, heading not just to Nashville but toward an event full of unknown danger.

Wait...

Maybe it wasn't so unknown.

A notion flitted through her mind, just a single word. She turned to Egly for confirmation.

"'Bold,'" she said. "That's it, isn't it? That's what you're up to. 'Bold.'"

Egly laughed again, nodding enthusiastically.

"You got it!"

Chelsi now knew what Egly was planning for Nashville.

And she nearly vomited.

# CHAPTER THIRTY-THREE

*Jacksonville, Florida*

CONNOR STOOD at the granite steps of the luxurious hotel in downtown Jacksonville, fighting the urge to grab the pack of cigarettes from his jacket pocket.

The view in front of him was all cloth—the backside of Octavius Osgood's linen suit jacket as well the shirts and jackets and pants and shoes of a crowd packed tightly around them. The people immediately surrounding them were members of the security team, whereas the glut of people beyond them were all members of the press. Notepads. Cameras. Pointing fingers.

As soon as Connor and the others had stepped out of the elevator into the marble lobby a few minutes earlier, he had seen the media waiting on the other side of the glass revolving doors. The moment they'd stepped outside, the media pounced all over them.

Word had spread.

Somebody, somewhere, somehow had learned of Chelsi's

disappearance. It hadn't taken long for the journalists to sniff out the rumors.

Damn media.

Osgood's girth continued to lead them down the steps to the waiting limousine below. The man was slow enough as it was, but in the current situation, he was positively glacial. In fact, the bone color of his linen suit stretched over his bowling ball physique made him look rather like an actual glacier waddling ever downward, step by step.

He'd immediately taken the lead position, and he'd also immediately assumed command of fielding all the questions. As if it wasn't humiliating enough to be following him, Osgood kept turning around and giving Connor huge grins that beamed past the oversized sunglasses and through the perfectly trimmed beard. He even placed a hand on Connor's shoulder a couple of times. Connor's sister was missing, and yet he *still* seemed to be enjoying the media attention.

That notion flashed through Connor's mind again, vying for clarity over his misplaced frustration with Osgood.

*Your sister is missing*, a part of him said in a voice that begged for reason.

Despite the deep-rooted guilt and concern that had been toying with Connor's conscience, he found himself desperately grasping onto a thread of hope. It was a fragile belief, one he repeated to himself like a mantra: *Chelsi is safe*. He repeated it over and over again, as if the sheer force of his conviction could will it into reality.

Deep down, he knew it was a coping mechanism, a way to shield himself from the overwhelming fear and uncertainty. In the absence of concrete information, he clung to the notion that his sister was out there somewhere, unharmed and waiting to be found. It was a fragile illusion, but it was the only anchor he had.

Reluctantly, Connor had to acknowledge a sliver of comfort that had settled within his anxious heart—the fact that it seemed Chelsi was with her new, mysterious companion, Zack. If anyone could ensure Chelsi's safety in this tumultuous time, it would be Zack. Despite his initial reservations and lingering distrust, Connor recognized that his earlier skepticism had been fueled by foolish pride and unwarranted suspicion. Zack hadn't brought chaos to Jacksonville; he'd tried to stop it. Zack had earned Connor's trust, and now Connor clung to the hope that his sister was indeed in the capable hands of the shadowy brute.

Osgood, Connor, and the security staff continued to slowly push their way through the crowd of reporters. The clamor of questions filled the air, drowning out the distant sounds of traffic. The reporters kept pushing in from all sides, their cameras flashing, microphones thrusting toward Osgood, who never missed a beat as his voice cut through the chaos, solid and confident, tinged with his thick Louisiana accent.

"Mr. Osgood," a female reporter shouted over the others, "is it true that Chelsi Nichols has been abducted?"

Osgood's gaze swept over the crowd, his expression calm and composed as he took another step down, his girth shaking. He raised a hand to silence the reporters and said, "I assure you, that's nothing more than a baseless rumor. Chelsi is safe and sound."

Connor clenched his jaw, his resentment simmering beneath the surface. He hated playing second fiddle to Osgood, being dragged around like a puppet on a string. The power he once believed he had within Chelsi's inner circle was slipping through his fingers.

As Osgood maneuvered through the throng of reporters, the questions continued to rain down upon him.

"So Chelsi will definitely be in Nashville tonight for the

Fourth of July concert?" one reporter shouted, pushing forward with a microphone in hand.

Another yelled, "And what about the first responders ceremony? That's Chelsi's favorite charity. Will it be postponed?"

The rest of the journalists joined in, their voices becoming a unified chorus of fervent questions.

Osgood took another step down. His belly jiggled again. He raised a hand, and his response was smooth, the distinctive accent oozing with confidence.

"Absolutely. The Nashville show will proceed as planned. You know Chelsi. Nothing's going to deter her from honoring the brave men and women who risk their lives for us every day."

Connor's gaze shifted, his eyes scanning the crowd of reporters. He could feel their scrutiny, their expectations weighing heavily upon the Chelsi Nichols contingent. At that moment, he despised his role as the silent figure in the shadows, his influence waning with each passing second.

As Osgood, Connor, and the security staff reached the awaiting limousine, the reporters continued their relentless assault, firing off questions like bullets.

"Now, don't you be worrying about any of that," Osgood said. "Just come on up to Nashville, and you can see for yourself."

With that, he shifted his mass through the open door and into the back of the limousine. Connor followed.

The soft leather seats were cool to the touch. There was a mini-bar with bottles of wine and champagne and glasses ready to be filled. The windows were tinted, and the carpet was deep and plush.

Connor reached into his jacket pocket, took out his pack of cigarettes, and bounced it between his hands. Of course, he wanted to light up. But Osgood wouldn't have it. He hated cigarettes. Loved cigars but hated cigarettes. Hypocrite.

Watching the pack of cigarettes move between his palms and recognizing that the only reason he wasn't lighting up was the other man's power only amplified the pathetic feelings of subservience that were already coursing through Connor. He shoved the pack back into his pocket.

His brain was spinning as frustration and envy battled within him. It should have been *him* a few moments ago, getting all the attention, speaking to the crowd with his definitive words and a commanding aura about Chelsi's current predicament. But instead, he found himself following Osgood, a passive witness of his own sister's story.

Osgood turned to Connor, his eyes glinting with authority and satisfaction. Connor could almost hear the unspoken message: *Know your place*.

The door closed behind them, muffling the cacophony of the reporters outside.

Connor felt his cheeks flushing red. His jaw clenched, and he nearly said something when...

A sudden pang of guilt shot through his core like a lightning bolt, shattering his cloud of self-centeredness.

Chelsi. His sister. Missing.

The realization instantly sobered his thoughts. All the petty desires for control and attention faded into insignificance as he confronted the harsh reality of Chelsi's absence. In that moment, he couldn't help but feel a profound sense of guilt for allowing his own ambitions to overshadow the genuine concern he should have felt for his sister's well-being.

The image of Chelsi's radiant smile and infectious laughter flashed through his mind. So, too, did the bond they shared since childhood. They had been each other's support, their pillars of strength through thick and thin. Connor couldn't fathom a world without Chelsi, and the mere thought of her in danger sent a sudden wave of panic through him.

To calm himself, he thought of one of his favorite memories—their first performance at the Holly Morton Theater. He could still feel the exhilaration as he and Chelsi stood side by side, ready to take the stage at the Holly Morton Theater. They were just children then. Ten and eight years old. Connor had gripped his miniature guitar tightly, his fingers tingling with nerves and excitement. Chelsi, even then, had been radiant and full of spirit.

When she stood before the microphone, her tiny stature already carried the promise of a star. But when she sang, that's when it *really* happened. From that very first note belting out into a dusty old theater in Hattiesburg, Mississippi, Connor knew he was witnessing something special. When the spotlight bathed them both in its warm glow, he recognized, even as an eight-year-old boy, that it belonged to Chelsi, not him.

With a sharp exhale, Connor came out of the memory, and suddenly things seemed clearer. Osgood was looking through the window, grinning. The reporters outside were yelling.

The limousine jerked to a gentle roll. In a moment, the noise of the reporters faded away.

As the limousine glided through the bustling streets, Connor's relief of a moment morphed into guilt.

*Chelsi is missing.*

His imagination conjured up a few awful images, throwing them at him in a flash.

*Zack is with her*, he reminded himself.

His hands clenched tightly, fingers digging into the armrest as his mind raced with unsettling possibilities. How could he have let his own thirst for power blind him to the real dangers lurking around Chelsi? He had been so consumed by his desire to assert control within her inner circle, to be at the forefront of her success, that he had neglected his most important role as her brother.

He couldn't change the past, but he could damn well make amends in the present. He would do whatever it took to find Chelsi, to ensure her safety, and to redeem himself from the selfish choices he had made.

# CHAPTER THIRTY-FOUR

*Hattiesburg, Mississippi*

SOMEHOW, Lenny had fallen into a subservient role.

As soon as Lenny had stepped out of the bathroom, Zack had instructed him to go through the contents of Egly's file box while Zack would continue exploring Egly's digital records on the laptop. Lenny had expected to find tax records, receipts, legal documents—all the stuff adults needed to keep track of. Instead, he found an assortment of Chelsi Nichols memorabilia: glossy photos of her on the Grammy red carpet, a poster from a concert, a program from a gala she held in honor of her charity work, teenager magazines.

A collection of obsession.

The sight of it all sent a pang through Lenny, an almost guilt-like feeling of silliness—he, too, was an adult mega-fan of Chelsi, and his collection of Chelsi Mae materials dwarfed this one in the plastic file box. He flushed at the thought of how ludicrous it must have looked to Zack.

"I haven't always been this way," he said and paused

momentarily. "I have money, and I wanted to spend it doing what *I* wanted to do, no matter what anyone else thought. That's why I started this groupie life. I've followed Chelsi Mae Nichols's tour for over two years now."

He turned and found Zack looking in his direction.

"Sometimes, though," Lenny continued, "it just feels ... I don't know. Wrong somehow."

He glanced down at the file box, saw Chelsi's smiling face beaming at him from atop a sun-drenched barrel in the middle of a pasture. A column of text was to her right. It was a page torn from a magazine—last summer's "Summertime Extravaganza" from *People*, if Lenny remembered correctly.

Ugh...

He exhaled.

Then he turned back to Zack. "For a while now, I've bounced the idea of doing something noble with my money. I want to establish a charity in Lima, Ohio, my hometown, something to help the needy and less fortunate. Is that silly?"

"No."

Lenny grinned. "Thanks."

"Finish what you..." Zack said and swallowed. "Started saying earlier."

It took Lenny a moment to remember. Before Zack's cellular rang, Lenny had started to tell him that Egly wasn't just another one of Chelsie's roadies.

"Egly and Chelsi must be friends," Lenny said. "A couple of years ago, paparazzi spotted them having coffee together. Big smiles. Big fun. I guess he's one of her 'inner circle' now."

Zack looked away from the laptop then and hummed thoughtfully.

Lenny continued going through the box, but as he rummaged through it. He noticed something he hadn't picked up on yet—an envelope tucked away in the back, behind all the folders. He pulled it out. It was thick, and something inside made it heavy.

For some reason, this made a chill flash over Lenny's flesh.

He slowly opened the envelope, peered inside...

...and gasped.

# CHAPTER THIRTY-FIVE

*Goodhope, Alabama*

EGLY HAD CHECKED the weather forecast several times, and all the experts were saying that it was gray and gloomy in Nashville. However, on Interstate 65, north of Birmingham, everything was sunny, green, and lush as it whooshed past the pickup truck.

Egly glanced over at Chelsi, her eyes fixed on the road ahead, her expression both stoic and frightened. He opened his mouth to speak but closed it. He paused for a moment, unsure what to say.

Finally, he said, "You're awfully quiet."

Still, Chelsi said nothing. She hadn't responded nor said anything at all for over an hour, but Egly was going to keep talking to her nonetheless.

Egly exhaled deeply, then glanced over—trying to make eye contact with her, trying to convey his sincerity—before he looked back to the road.

"Chel, baby. Sweeheart. I've dreamed of a beautiful future together, a future free of the violence and the dangers we've faced, where we can be together without fear. A world with no more debts to pay, with all the troubles of the past left behind and our lives starting anew."

He had tried to maintain a passionate tone, but still Chelsi said nothing. He turned to her, compassion in his eyes.

"To get us there," he said, "my blood debt must be completed. I'll have to exact it from the people in Nashville. They brought us so much suffering, and I can't let that stand." He reached over and squeezed her hand tightly and could feel the fear radiating from her body. He wanted to protect her then, no matter what it cost him.

"Think about it," he said. "We could have a little house in a nice, peaceful part of town, and have coffee together every morning. We could explore our city, go to cozy bars and restaurants at night ... so many days and nights full of joy and satisfaction. Wouldn't that be great?"

No reply

"Listen closely. A little extra blood-letting is all it'll take. I'm talking about a perfect war. A war that won't cause death or destruction but will *end* it all and bring permanent peace. It'll be so perfect, Chel, so complete in its effect on the world; the way we understand and interact with each other will never be the same again.

"Imagine a world without violence or hate. *Imagine it!*" he said, slamming his hand on the steering wheel. "Chel? Chel? *Chelsi!* Can't you envision it?"

And, again, *no damn reply*.

He looked over at her. Tears were streaming down her cheeks. She quaked.

Alarmed, Egly reached over and took her shoulder. "Honey, why are you crying?"

She finally moved, pulling away from him.

He leaned farther in her direction.

"Honey!"

"Stop!" she screamed. "*Stop!*"

Egly froze where he was. Then shrugged and resumed his position, sitting tall behind the wheel.

Hmph.

Women.

But despite the brief quarrel with his beloved, Egly smiled. Darkness surrounded their union, true. They were facing danger. Yet he held onto his optimism. As long as he was willing to pay the price in blood, he and Chelsi could have a perfect war and, with it, a perfect life together.

# CHAPTER THIRTY-SIX

*Hattiesburg, Mississippi*

SILENCE RUSHED UP TO WARD, standing behind him to look down at the envelope. It was full of photographs. Ward flipped through them.

Every one of the photos featured only two people: Chelsi and Egly.

Arms intertwined.

Their cheeks pressed together.

Eyes shining with contentment.

Chelsi's huge smile beaming.

In one moment, the truth was revealed.

Silence's breath was labored as he stared at the photographs in disbelief. Everything he had believed was being turned upside down. He had thought that Chelsi—the woman he had been trying to save—was the victim, but now it seemed they had been working in tandem.

"Looks like they were more than friends," Ward said softly, eyeing the photos with a mixture of awe and confusion.

Silence could only nod in agreement. Was this why Chelsi

had been so elusive? Was this why she had been so coy when answering his questions? He could feel bile rising in his throat.

"There's something else," Ward said. "Behind the photos."

He pulled out a slip of paper. It had two handwritten columns.

*young - dead*
*old - dead*
*broken - missed!*
*bold -*

Clearly, the list referred to the murders—two *dead*s, one *missed*, and one blank—but the other word...

"What the hell?" Silence said.

He ran the words through his brain.

*young, old, broken, bold*

Heather Winslow, the twelve-year-old girl, would be the *young* death, and the elderly woman in North Carolina was the *old*. Egly had planned on shooting a handicapped individual in Jacksonville—the *broken*—but what could—

"Hey!" Ward said. He was staring at Silence with an incredulous expression. "Come on! It's from the lyrics to 'Cabin Nights, City Lights.' 'The young, the old. The broken and the bold.'"

Silence nodded.

Yes, clearly. So *bold* might mean...

A detail flashed through Silence's mind.

"The concert tonight..." he said and swallowed. "There's a special event...?"

Ward's eyes widened. "There is!"

He fished into his satchel, pulled out a battered concert program and read aloud.

"'Nashville. Fourth of July. Pre-concert: Chelsi will be

hosting the Bold Hearts Ceremony to honor the nation's first responder heroes.'"

"The bold..." Silence said.

He looked away.

"Well, what are we going to do?" Ward said.

Silence turned back to him. "We have a plane to catch."

# CHAPTER THIRTY-SEVEN

*Nashville, Tennessee*

IT HAD BECOME PAINFULLY clear to Chelsi that Egly was more than just unhinged; he was surely under the influence of something.

Relevant memories from their brief interactions came flooding back to her. Two years ago, Egly had mentioned his past experimentations with drugs. He hadn't been specific, but he'd said he tried things more potent than marijuana.

But she would have never imagined Egly would be on anything *this* potent. He gripped the steering wheel so tightly that his knuckles whitened. His face was drenched in sweat, his eyes bloodshot, and a manic grin stretched across his face. An angry red patch had formed on the right side of his neck where he kept scratching at something, like a dog with a flea.

Holy shit. Chelsi didn't know what to expect. She'd never even smoked a joint! She sat in the passenger seat, her heart pounding against her chest.

Despite Egly's unsettling state, he had somehow managed to get them to their destination in one piece.

They'd made it to Nashville.

Ahead, through the windshield, was the Bear Grove Center arena. Its exterior was a striking blend of modern design and urban energy, a testament to the city's vibrant entertainment scene, and it commanded attention amidst the bustling streets. As the setting sun poked through the gray gloom clinging to the sky, the building's facade came alive, its outer walls, crafted with a combination of glass panels and polished steel.

As the truck pulled closer, Chelsi got a better view of the arena's massive parking lot, which was ablaze with artificial light. She saw the two outdoor setups in the massive parking lot, those that would host the pre-concert festivities. The first area was designated for tailgating, where plenty of pickups were already parked with tents and grills set up, the perfect warmup before heading into the arena.

On the opposite end of the space, the second location consisted of a large dais and a cordoned-off seating area where the Bold Hearts Ceremony would be held, an event dedicated to honoring first responders such as police officers, firefighters, paramedics, and dispatchers. Red, white, and blue balloons decorated the stage. Nearby were banners showcasing various heroes from different states along with their stories of courage and selflessness.

At a gate, Egly flashed one of Chelsi's high-level security cards to the uniformed guard. Egly had never had that level of clearance when he was her roadie; he must have gotten the card from his unknown partner. The guard seemed dubious at first, but when he saw Chelsi in the passenger seat, his eyes went wide. He smiled and waved them through without question.

Turning to her, Egly broke the tense quiet.

"You must be wondering who my partner has been all this

time," he said, raising the security pass and shaking it. His voice was tinged with a twisted sense of satisfaction.

Chelsi didn't respond.

But inside, she already knew the answer. Egly had been merely a pawn, a tool used by someone far more cunning and dangerous. The realization made Chelsi feel lightheaded, yet she maintained her composure, not wanting to reveal her suspicions prematurely.

Egly maneuvered the truck around the perimeter of the facility to a side loading dock designated for tractor trailers. Concrete walls. Fencing. The entrance is wide enough for a large semi-truck to pass through and was marked off by yellow-painted metal poles

Chelsi's eyes landed on a figure waiting there.

A massive bowl of a figure.

It was the exact person who'd crossed Chelsi's mind moments earlier when Egly asked her if she wondered who his partner was...

Octavius Osgood stood with his usual air of calculated confidence, smiling at the truck as its brakes squealed it to a gentle stop.

"Get out," Egly said.

Egly opened his door, walked around the truck, threw the passenger door open, and grabbed Chelsi's wrist.

"I said, get out!"

He pulled her outside. She stumbled, not taking her eyes off Osgood, who was elevated a few feet above them on the concrete landing. He never stopped smiling.

"You got a lot of blood debt left to pay off, boy," Osgood said. "You failed in Jax."

"I know, I know," Egly said and scratched at his neck. He looked at Chelsi, smiled warmly. "For her, I'll kill them, Big O."

Osgood chuckled. "Let's hope you don't have to." He fixed his eyes on Chelsi before continuing. "That is, if she's compliant."

Chelsi had no idea what that meant. But it sounded bad.

And it also brought up some bad memories...

Osgood pointed at the truck. "Well, go on, now. Get ready." He took a walkie-talkie from his belt, waved it. "I'll let you know what the plan is."

Egly nodded, gave one more warm, longing glance at Chelsi, and then went back to the truck. A moment later, it started off.

"Come here, Chelsi," Osgood said.

She cautiously ascended the three steps to the concrete landing. Her heart raced.

He slipped his hands around her shoulders and looked into her eyes, a deceptive gentleness to his touch.

"You want to know why I'm here?"

Chelsi nodded, barely able to speak.

Osgood grinned. "Malcolm Egly's been my soldier. My mercenary, killing the fans of country music sensation, Chelsi Mae Nichols. If I create enough chaos and distrust around the Chelsi Nichols brand, no one will believe her claims if she blows the whistle on me, the relentless promoter who's put every ounce of his energy into branding and promoting Chelsi Nichols for three years."

His lips curled into a cruel smirk as he continued.

"What that girl said about me six months ago could *ruin* me, Chelsi Mae. You're the It Girl. America's Sweetheart. If everyone's favorite girl next door goes on public record corroborating the little bitch's claims, they'll believe anything you say."

He paused to run a hand over his beard.

"Well, they *would have* believed anything you said. They

might not if everyone who comes near you keeps dying. The first two were a warmup. It's going to be a bloodbath tonight."

He pointed in the direction where Egly had just disappeared.

"Why Egly?" Chelsi said.

Osgood scoffed.

"Because he's a nut. You were nice enough to have coffee with him a couple times two years ago, and he's believed the two of you are star-crossed lovers since. Haven't I told you not to be so trusting?"

She scowled. "Yeah. You told me that, all right. *Eventually*."

The corner of Osgood's mouth lifted. He put his massive hand back on her shoulder. And rubbed. Just so.

She yanked away from him.

Another scoff from Osgood. "Egly also has a drug problem. I didn't tell you that's why I fired him. Now I'm feeding him fentanyl and playing with his other favorite vice: superstition. He's convinced I'm some sort of voodoo master because of the New Orleans accent."

He laughed.

"So I got the guy out of his mind on the poison, thinking if he pays off a 'blood debt' he can have you forever. And he will. I'm a man of my word. I'll make sure he gets paid."

Chelsi looked away from him.

"Now..." Osgood said, letting the word float in the air for a moment. "Egly's out there at your beloved first responders event setting up phosgene gas that will be released on my command." He showed her the walkie talkie again. "You can have dozens of good people's blood on your hands along with a ruined career along with a nutcase boyfriend who'll probably kill you. Orrrrr, you can simply agree that you won't go on TV and corroborate the girl's claims."

He put a finger under her chin, tilted her head up to look him eye to eye.

"I'll give you a few minutes to think it over," he whispered.

# CHAPTER THIRTY-EIGHT

SILENCE DRUMMED his fingers on the leather armrest.

His gaze shifted to the window, where a sea of clouds was visible. Although Nashville was expecting overcast gloom, it looked bright and clear in the higher altitude.

The hum of the Learjet's engines took on a different tone, and Silence felt a slight drop as the plane began its descent. Ward sat across from him in a matching black leather seat. Since leaving Hattiesburg, Ward had grown quiet and withdrawn, only saying a few words. As with the hotel room, Ward gave no reaction to the luxuries of the high-end aircraft; he was neither impressed nor ungrateful.

Silence mulled over Egly and Chelsi's upcoming attack—some sort of attack on the Bold Hearts Ceremony tribute to American first responders. Whatever they had planned, Silence could only assume that since they were specifically targeting the event that came immediately *before* Chelsi's concert, they intended the attack to be a mass murder. It was the final show of Chelsi's tour. The couple was going to end their killing spree with a bang on the Fourth of July.

Silence thought about the people who were being honored at the event, the people who could be murdered—police, firefighters, dispatchers, EMTs...

Some of the best individuals humanity had to offer ... about to be slaughtered.

He pushed the notion away, attempting to pivot his attention elsewhere, but the nagging thought that replaced it was just as bad.

It presented itself as a single image.

A beautiful, smiling face with untamable red hair.

Chelsi Mae Nichols.

Silence hated himself for believing the image she presented, that of a wholesome, all-American girl with love in her heart and gold in her voice.

His fingers clenched tighter on the armrest.

For a moment, he thought C.C.'s voice was going to call to him, but he cut her off at the pass. He didn't need C.C.'s help recognizing his emotional reaction.

He took a deep breath, released it. And also released his grip on the armrest.

Time to refocus. Time for rationality.

But as he searched for logical meaning, he found nothing. His mind kept looping on a single-word question: *Why?*

Extrapolating that simple query only sent into further mental loops.

Why was Chelsi doing this?

Why kill her own fans?

Why bring about chaos on her concert tour?

It just didn't make sense.

That is, it didn't make sense until Silence thought of Egly's sneering face. The man was entirely deranged. And Chelsi was his lover.

Which meant she was likely entirely insane as well.

Silence shook his head, disgusted at himself. He'd believed the beaming smile, the lil ol' accent, the tender lyrics.

Just like he'd believed Slick Chambers in Sioux City.

Dozens of people's lives were at risk down there in Nashville. And because Silence hadn't been vigilant, it was his fault.

# CHAPTER THIRTY-NINE

THE FUN WAS ABOUT to begin.

Egly pulled the truck to a stop beside the massive dais, where polo-shirt-wearing Bear Grove workers were putting the finishing touches on the Bold Hearts Ceremony. It was only twenty minutes until the main event, and people were already filing into the rows of folding chairs facing the stage. A few dignitaries had arrived, too, wearing their cop or fire-fighter or whatever uniforms. At the front of the stage, tall speakers had been erected, projecting a joyous song—one of Chelsi's, of course—in anticipation of the event.

It made him think of her. The song.

He had a vision of himself and Chelsi standing victorious amongst the rubble of a battle, holding each other's hands with a look of unbreakable determination on their faces. Drenched in blood. He could see them in matching uniforms, gleaming weapons in their hands, their love for each other always unwavering.

Wars and love.

Wars and blood.

Blood and love.

He scratched at his neck.

That damn bug wouldn't piss off!

A fat woman waddled down the set of metal steps off the stage and leaned into his open window. She didn't frown, but she was clearly flustered at being interrupted only minutes before the event.

"Are you with NPD?"

"Huh?" Egly said. "No, I got the fireworks."

He hooked a thumb over his shoulder toward the tarp in the back.

"Fireworks? We already have fireworks."

She gestured toward the metal stands on either side of the stage, each of which was loaded with boxes that looked identical to those under the tarp in Egly's truck.

"Oh jeez..." Egly said and let out a fake sigh. "They didn't call, did they?"

The woman just looked at him.

Egly reached under the seat and pulled out a clipboard. Entirely legitimate. Osgood had provided it. He handed it to the woman.

"Fire marshal," he said with a whatcha-gonna-do shrug. "Those old ones gotta be changed. Some sort of recall."

The woman groaned as she read over the memo. She took another look back to the stage, whistled, and waved down a pair of teenage boys wearing shirts that matched hers.

"I guess I can't complain too much," she said and pointed to the banner: *BOLD HEARTS CEREMONY*. "The fire marshal is part of the first responder community."

Egly's truck rocked gently as the boys began uncovering the boxes behind him.

"That's the spirit," Egly said and scratched his neck.

# CHAPTER FORTY

THE CAR'S brakes screeched as Silence brought it to an abrupt halt and jumped out. It was the Cadillac he picked up at the Nashville airport, his third set of wheels in as many days.

Ward disembarked from the passenger side and met Silence by the front of the vehicle. Ahead was the Bold Hearts Ceremony—a sprawling stage at the eastern edge of the Bear Grove parking area, cordoned off by stanchions and velvet ropes. The rows of folding chairs were nearly at full capacity, and the stage was full of dignified-looking individuals in dress uniforms speaking to each other and laughing.

Silence and Ward rushed toward the ceremony without exchanging a word, weaving through the loiterers on the periphery of the action. These people's tranquil chatter clashed with the imminent danger Silence knew was about to unfold.

If only Silence knew *how* the danger was going to unfold.

His eyes scanned the scene, roaming over the ceremony. He brought his attention to the vibrant colors of the uniforms of the first responders on the stage, then moved to the spectators in their neat rows of folding chairs. His gaze paused on each individual, looking for any hint of danger.

Maybe if he...

There.

Shit, there he was.

A white pickup was beside the stage, and Egly was behind the wheel, waiting as a pair of teenagers in matching polo shirts frowned at a tarp they were struggling to untie from the truck's bed.

Egly waited with a grin, an arm stuck out the open driver-side door. With one hand, he drummed the truck's mirror; he scratched his neck with the other. But when his gaze shifted slightly and he saw Silence, the smile dropped, and his eyes went wide.

Immediately, Egly threw his door open, said something hurriedly to the woman supervising the teenagers, and bolted away.

Silence's thighs instantly tensed as he nearly sprinted off after Egly.

But he didn't move.

His eyes remained on the load that the teenagers had just unloaded.

He turned to Ward.

"There's something awful..." he said and swallowed. "In those boxes."

Silence looked at Egly—getting farther away, not slowing at all from his run—and the boxes.

He couldn't let the murderer go, but he couldn't leave the boxes either.

His mind threatened to spiral out of control on him.

But then Ward said, "Go get Egly." He pointed at the boxes. "I'll stop this."

Silence hesitated.

Only hours ago, he'd taken one look at this man and

assumed he was some sort of deadbeat. Since then, he'd discovered that Ward was a well-off, if not troubled, man with a heart of gold and some real grit.

He stole another look at Egly.

Nearing a corner by an outer structure.

About to disappear.

Silence spun back on Ward. "Okay."

He sprinted after Egly.

# CHAPTER FORTY-ONE

LENNY'S FEET ached as he sprinted towards the official-looking woman standing by the pickup truck. He hadn't run this hard in years.

His mind was racing with urgency. Breathless, he reached the woman's side.

"There's something bad in those boxes," Lenny blurted out, his voice filled with urgency.

The woman looked at him, her expression a mix of confusion and revulsion. Her eyes darted between the boxes and Lenny, trying to make sense of his frantic plea.

"*What's* in them?" she said, her tone tinged with doubt. Despite her dubious tone, she took a step to the side, distancing herself from the boxes.

Lenny hesitated for a moment. He knew something awful was about to happen if he didn't stop it, but all the same, he had no answer for the woman.

"I don't know," he admitted. "But, listen, that guy who just dropped them off is the guy who killed the people in Virginia and North Carolina."

The woman inched away. "I think you need to leave. Please. Or I'm gonna call security."

Lenny's heart sank as he realized the limited time he had to reason with her. He wanted to explain the urgency, the potential danger that lurked within those boxes, but he knew he had little time to change her mind. Frustration welled up within him as he tried to formulate a plan.

"I get it," he said. "This sounds crazy. But, please, lives are at stake!"

The woman eyed him and stepped farther away as she brought a radio to her mouth.

Time seemed to slip away, each passing second intensifying the weight of the impending danger. Lenny's mind raced with the need to act, to find a way to avert disaster.

# CHAPTER FORTY-TWO

SILENCE'S FOOTSTEPS thundered off the concrete walls within the intricate corridors at the rear of the Bear Grove facility. Egly had slipped away after his head start had given him a significant advantage, but Silence refused to let him escape.

Plus, it always helps to have an ace up your sleeve.

Silence had studied the facility's layout upon entering and made a rough visual outline in his mind, something that harkened back to his initial training with the Watchers. Bear Grove's only viable escape route was to the east. With that knowledge, Silence wagered that if he cut through the auxiliary buildings to the side, he could intercept Egly before he fled the grounds.

That was the plan, anyway.

Turning a corner, Silence plunged deeper into the rear structures of the arena. The bowels of the building seemed to swallow him whole as he navigated the maze-like passageways. The air grew stale, and the overhead lights flickered intermittently, casting eerie shadows on the gray walls. A distant sound of footsteps—Egly's, of course—echoed through the labyrinthine corridors, blending with the racing thoughts in Silence's mind.

As he sprinted past a loading dock, Silence did a double-take. It wasn't Egly he spotted, but it *was* a person. Two of them, actually. He knew them both, and the site made his heart pulse even faster than it already was.

There, in the harsh fluorescent glow, he saw Chelsi with Octavius Osgood looming over her, clasping her by the wrist.

The realization struck Silence with a jolt—Chelsi wasn't the mastermind behind this nefarious plot; she was a captive, another victim, perhaps *the* victim.

He had misjudged Chelsi.

At the sight of Silence, Osgood's eyes widened with alarm. He released his grip on Chelsi and sprinted away as fast as his bulbous legs could carry him, slipping into the shadows.

"Coward," Silence growled under his breath in spite of the pain in his throat.

He watched until Osgood disappeared, but he never broke his stride, never slowing from a sprint.

Silence's focus narrowed. He couldn't let Osgood escape, but neither could he let Egly escape. Egly had admitted to killing Heather Winslow. That was enough for Silence to chase after him.

Besides, Osgood would be easy enough to catch up with later. A famous man like Osgood couldn't hide in a world this small.

Chelsi stood there alone, in the middle of the landing, free from her captor. Their eyes locked for an instant as Silence ran past. It was some sort of unspoken acknowledgment, a shared understanding.

As Silence turned a corner, Chelsi was wiped from his vision.

He pressed on, sprinting harder.

# CHAPTER FORTY-THREE

LENNY STARED at the foreboding boxes, frozen in place. He hadn't hesitated when he told Zack to chase after Egly and let Lenny handle the situation at the truck.

Now Lenny had a horrible feeling he should have let Zack handle everything.

He wracked his brain for a way to confirm his suspicions without endangering himself or others. Several yards away now, the woman held true to her promise; she was speaking frantically into her radio, calling for security, casting occasional fretful glances in Lenny's direction.

Time was slipping away. Whatever was in those boxes could be set to timers. Lenny's eyes darted, searching for a solution. Then, a bold idea sparked in his mind.

Just attack the situation head-on.

With steady hands, he approached one of the boxes and crouched beside it. Gently, oh-so-gently, he grasped the edge of the lid and began to peel it back.

As the lid lifted, Lenny exhaled at the good news: the box didn't explode in his face.

But the bad news quickly negated any relief.

Nestled within the box were vials filled with a sinister-looking liquid, their labels hinting at their lethal nature. Intricate wiring lay alongside them, unmistakably some sort of detonation system.

He turned to the woman. "Look! Believe me now?"

At first, the woman scowled. Then her eyes abruptly opened wide. She hurried over.

"Oh ... my God," she said.

Lenny eased the lid closed, stood up, and moved closer to her.

"You have to evacuate the area," he said under his breath. "Quietly! We don't know how these things are triggered. A panicked stampede could set them off."

She looked at the crowd and back to Lenny. "You're right."

She moved away, getting back on her radio and speaking in a hushed tone.

And Lenny exhaled.

# CHAPTER FORTY-FOUR

EGLY SCRAMBLED down the metal stairs, going to the parking lot below. There was the pickup truck, where he'd left it by the ceremony with the fat bitch and her teenaged helpers. Egly had sent Zack on a wild goose chase through the outer structure of Bear Grove, making him think he was going for the exit. Really, he was looping them all the way back to the truck.

But he had to get there fast. He'd managed to elude Zack for some time, but in the last few moments, Zack was right behind him.

And gaining.

Zack's footsteps pounded on the platform behind, coming at a run.

Egly made it to the ground level and clambered off, his feet scuffling on the blacktop.

*Clang! Clang! Clang!*

He looked back.

There was Zack, streaking down the stairs, his large feet making resonant thuds on the steps.

Shit! How had Zack closed the gap so quickly?

No time to worry about that now. The pickup truck was ahead, its white siding glowing brightly in the darkness at the edge of the parking lot. Egly bolted for it, yanked open the door, entered, fired it up.

The tires chirped as he took off.

A glance in the rearview.

There was Zack. Running at full speed.

*...and still closing the gap.*

Egly floored the gas pedal, and the truck's engine whined as he gained momentum. Yanking the steering wheeled to the right, he barreled around a row of cars, tires screeching. A few stray concert-goers screamed at him, called him a maniac.

He didn't give a shit about *those* concert-goers, however.

Egly had on his mind the people on the other side of the parking lot...

Osgood had promised Egly that if he completed the assignments, he could make Chelsi love him. Egly had been successful in his first two kills, but he missed his mark in Jacksonville. Now, as he faced his most important mission yet —mass murder in Nashville—Egly knew that the poison gas hadn't worked.

But he could salvage this.

He could still commit Osgood's mass murder.

Egly closed his eyes. He pictured Chelsi's beaming smile, beautiful eyes, and that wild hair that had captured the hearts of the entire county and much of the world. For two magical nights, she'd been his.

And if he could keep this truck on course, she could be his again. Forever, this time.

He clenched the steering wheel tighter and pulled around another aisle of cars, not checking for oncoming vehicles, nearly clipping a Celica. More people screamed at him.

Another glance at the rearview mirror.

Dammit, there he was! Zack!

Egly had peeled around two corners, barely taking his foot off the gas, and there was Zack, still behind him, still at a full sprint, still closing the distance between them.

Fuming, Egly looked back to the windshield.

And immediately the scowl left his face, replaced with a smile.

There was the tailgating area. Just ahead. The new destination. Egly was almost there.

Bright, artificial lighting flooded the area, and the logos of various corporate sponsors were emblazoned larger-than-life all around. People had gathered amongst pickup trucks wearing Chelsi Nichols T-shirts. There were copious red plastic cups filled with beer and people talked, laughed, and enjoyed themselves. Some people pointed in his direction, but most of the pointers were laughing, clearly thinking the truck was some sort of prank. They didn't yet understand the danger they were in.

They couldn't possibly comprehend that a pickup truck was about to plow through them.

Egly checked the rearview mirror again.

Zack was close behind, pounding the pavement with every ounce of energy he had. He was approaching fast.

Only yards away.

Then feet away.

Then...

*Thump!*

Zack jumped onto the back of the truck, both arms hooked over the tailgate. He looked forward, right into the mirror, looking directly at Egly. In the reflection, their eyes locked.

Somehow, Zack's ever-stoic expression registered even more cold precision than usual. It let Egly know something...

Zack meant to kill him.

It was now or never.

Egly's knuckles whitened as he grasped the wheel tightly and turned it left, then right in rapid succession, the truck jerking and skidding across the blacktop. Zack clung on, his arms taut and rigid.

Egly smashed the accelerator, and the engine roared in protest. Sweat beaded on Egly's forehead as he took sharp turns, slammed on his brakes, and even attempted drifting around corners with zero success.

Zack held on the whole time, refusing to let go.

In the chaos of trying to shake Zack, Egly had turned them all the way around, heading in the opposite direction of the tailgating area. He yanked the wheel left, bringing the truck back around. The tires screeched. The smell of burnt rubber filled the cab.

The tailgating area appeared ahead. Much closer.

*Now* the people realized the danger they were in. There were screams. Thrown lawn chairs. Pickup trucks firing up.

To hell with Zack and the interruption he posed. As long as Zack didn't make it off the tailgate and up the bed of the truck to the cab, Egly could deal with Zack *after* he'd plowed through the crowd. So he simply needed to...

Shit!

Another look at the rearview mirror revealed Zack had somehow pulled his massive frame over the tailgate and was crawling up the bed, only a couple of feet from the cab.

Luckily, Egly always had a contingency item.

He reached under the seat, and the truck's wheels screeched louder as it yanked to the side. His fingers explored, feeling the grimy carpet, searching for...

Metal!

There it was.

The can of pepper spray.

# CHAPTER FORTY-FIVE

Silence's hands were on fire as he clung onto the back of the pickup truck. Egly had attempted to throw him off by quickly swerving left and right, but he'd held on. His muscles, too, ached from the strain.

The truck continued toward the panicked tailgating zone, and Egly pushed forward in a straight path, gunning the engine.

And that gave Silence his chance.

He spread his legs to the edges of the truck's bed, stabilizing himself, and grabbed onto the roof. With a heave of his torso, he fought against the truck's momentum and the rush of wind and swung an elbow straight through the rear window.

*Crash!*

The glass shattered.

The impact sent a wave of pain through Silence's arm, but he reaffirmed his grip on the slippery metal of the truck's roof, momentarily regained his balance...

...and then pounced.

Putting all his power into his back legs, he shot his entire frame forward, folding in on himself, creating all the clearance he could for his massive shoulders and long legs. He shot through the hole he'd busted in the glass, its jagged shards tearing at his clothes.

Silence bashed into the truck's dash, and he regained his bearings in time to see the headliner above him, along with Egly's sneering face and some sort of can, which was pointed in Silence's direction.

In a fraction of a second, the mystery of the can was solved.

It was pepper spray.

A stream shot in Silence's direction. His reflexes were honed to scalpel precision—through his Watchers training as well as years of real-world experience—so his arm shot up with plenty of time, blocking the stream. But while his reflexes were timely, there was only so much a forearm could do to block a steady stream of pepper spray.

Egly sprayed non-stop, causing the liquid to splash across Silence and the inside of the truck. Despite closing his eyes tightly, Silence felt the liquid splatter all over his face, and he sensed a small amount trickle through the tight line of his eyelids.

That was all it took.

Silence's face contorted in agony as fluid streamed from his eyes and nose. His chest contracted with deep inhales, gasping for breath. He blinked rapidly, trying to clear his vision as he swiped at Egly.

The tires screeched, and centrifugal force shot Silence to the side of the truck, where he bashed into the passenger door.

Screams from outside.

Close.

They were almost to the tailgaters.

Silence gritted his teeth and forced his eyes open, fraction of inch by fraction of an inch, until he saw Egly—both hands on the wheel now, done with the expended pepper spray can —cackling as he leaned toward the windshield. The engine roared.

More of Silence's training, as well as his instincts, kicked in. Lives were at stake. With a surge of adrenaline, Silence reached out half-blindly and grabbed Egly's shoulder, yanked. Silence's eyes involuntarily pinched shut again. The truck's tires screeched as it jolted to the side. Egly pummeled Silence's shoulders, his head.

Again, Silence willed his eyes open. Tears poured down his cheeks. There was Egly. Laughing. Punching. Silence focused on the steering wheel.

Reached.

Missed.

Reached.

And caught hold.

He yanked it hard, causing the tires to screech as the truck rocked on its suspension. Outside, people screamed.

The truck was still heading right for the tailgaters. Despite their efforts to flee, their panic was causing them to clump up. There were too damn many of them.

Tugging on the steering wheel hadn't worked.

So Silence needed to go the more direct route.

C.C.'s voice came to him, concerned. *Love, what are you doing?*

He ignored her. Blindly, he launched himself in the opposite direction of the cab, barreling into Egly and knocking him off balance. The truck lurched to the side with Egly's sudden jerk on the steering wheel.

Silence felt the truck start to tip. He had only a fraction of a second before the whole thing toppled over. Silence tucked himself into a ball without hesitation, curled his arms around his head, and dove toward the side of the truck that was lifting up—the least dangerous direction for him.

The crash came in slow motion as the truck rolled several times.

*Crunch-thump!*
*Crunch-thump!*
*Crunch-thump!*

Every square inch of Silence was bombarded with metal and glass. People screamed from outside. And the truck rolled and rolled.

Then Silence heard a sickening thud. His body smashed into the steering column as the truck came to a dead stop plastered against a parked vehicle.

He forced open his eyes. It felt like razor blades were scratching across his corneas. Fighting hard against the squinting, he saw that Egly hadn't faired as well in the crash.

The mangled body lay only inches away from Silence, the face twisted into a horrific mask of pain and terror, one arm reaching out as if Egly were trying to grab hold of something just out of reach. His eyes were empty and still. The stench of feces filled Silence's nostrils as he stared through the tears at the other man's remains.

Silence strained to peer through his slitted eyelids, through the relentless, pepper-spray-induced tears, through the destroyed windshield, and to the parking lot.

The truck had stopped several yards away from the tail-gaters. They were safe.

Silence had stopped the bastard in time.

He heard sirens in the distance.

Shit!

Silence fought against the disorienting pain in his eyes. They shut, wouldn't reopen. The twisted metal and shattered glass surrounding him formed a treacherous obstacle course.

Undeterred, he went into motion, his every movement guided by instinct and sheer willpower.

With each inch, his hands reached out, carefully navigating the jagged edges of the ruined pickup. He felt the crumpled metal, sharp fragments, torn cloth. In his blindness, he thought of Mrs. Enfield and how her remaining four senses sometimes seemed to be heightened; he relied on touch and intuition to guide him through the tangled debris.

Finally, his groping fingers found the door. It was a mangled, misshapen mess of metal and plastic, bent inward. And it wouldn't move. Silence pulled back, rammed his shoulder into it.

*Screeeeech!*

The door's ruined hinges howled, and a gust of fresh air rushed into the cab. Silence probed around until he found the edges of the door frame and then pulled himself into the parking lot, where he collapsed into a heap.

A deep breath.

And another.

But there was no time to recover; the sirens were louder now. Much louder. Closer. As Silence forced his eyelids open a fraction of an inch, red-and-blue flashing lights lit up his blurry vision.

With one last burst of energy, he sprinted away.

# CHAPTER FORTY-SIX

SOMETIMES, things are just meant to be.

Including concerts.

An hour had passed since the two potential concert-spoilers had occurred outside Bear Grove Center arena: the unfortunate cancellation of the Bold Heart Ceremony due to unforeseen technical difficulties with sound equipment, as well as a runaway truck that was stopped by a Good Samaritan who slipped away without taking credit.

Many performers would have canceled their shows.

But not Chelsi Nichols.

Silence and Ward were seated in lawn chairs among the resilient non-ticket-holding tailgaters who had braved the possibility of another runaway truck. Silence had bought a hotdog. He needed one after the shit he'd gone through that night. He bought one for Ward, too. Ward had also gone through some shit.

The atmosphere in the rather depleted tailgating area was a mix of relief and excitement, a sense of camaraderie forged by their shared experience. The aroma of grilled food filled the air, blending with the lingering scent of burnt rubber and automobile exhaust.

As they sat side by side, the fans surrounding them chattered, recounting the events and exchanging their own versions of the near-disaster. Laughter and applause intermittently erupted. Silence pushed the last bite of hotdog into his mouth. A little normalcy was delicious after all the chaos.

The arena loomed over it all, lit up brilliantly against the night. Though she couldn't be heard outside, Chelsi was in there doing her work. And after getting to know her, Silence was sure she was singing with every bit of her soul.

Besides Silence, Ward was also finishing up his hotdog. He gave Silence a nod and said, "Thanks again."

Silence nodded back.

He anticipated Ward would say something else, some poignant words for a poignant moment. Maybe he'd elaborate on his dream of starting a charity.

But he said nothing.

Silence appreciated that. Ward was a good dude. He had it where it counted.

So instead of chatting, they listened to Chelsi singing through a dozen different radios, many of them playing "Cabin Nights, City Lights."

Silence had never cared for country music, but this was something special. He was glad to be listening to it.

———

Bear Grove Center's green room bore a different color palette than the one in Jacksonville. It was a bit smaller but a lot newer. The smell of brand-new furniture filled the air, mixed with the scent of Chelsi's makeup, hairspray, and post-concert sweat.

Silence and Chelsi were alone in the room. Chelsi wore an

oversized robe over her last stage outfit. They faced each other on a pair of blue-upholstered sofas.

Chelsi's gaze was lost in the distance. She cradled a cup of iced mint tea over her crossed legs. She looked every inch a superstar, while she was also the picture of humble strength. Wearied. Resilient.

"After chaos..." Silence said and swallowed. "And with Osgood missing..." Another swallow. "You still got on stage." Another swallow. "Impressive."

Chelsi pulled her attention from whatever distant thought she was musing on and gave him a faint smile.

"The show must go on."

"I'm sorry..." He swallowed. "I doubted you."

Chelsi put her hand to her chest and opened her eyes wide in a show of dramatic offense. Using an over-the-top rendition of her Southern accent, she said, "My stars, I just can't believe you suspected lil ol' Chelsi Mae!"

She smiled.

Silence grinned.

In her normal voice, she added, "Don't worry about it. Anyone would have come to the same conclusion. I hung out with Egly twice two years ago. I guess you might call them dates. Maybe... He was a sweet guy then. I just wanted to get to know him. He insisted on those photos, and to be honest, they kind of creeped me out."

She glanced down and tapped her fingernails on her glass.

"Osgood..." she said. "Do you think he—"

"He'll be handled."

"But—"

"He'll be handled," Silence repeated.

"That's why all of this happened," she said quietly, looking back at the space on the wall she'd been studying earlier. "When I was first getting started, he approached me. It seemed amazing at first, having someone that famous interested in promoting *me*. But soon I found that he wanted ... a favor. And..." She trailed off. Paused. "Not intercourse, but ... a favor. And I complied. Twice. Told him I wouldn't again. "

She looked up at him, gave a sad smirk.

"Betcha don't think I'm the all-American sweetheart now, huh?"

"Life's tricky," Silence said and swallowed.

Silence sure as hell wouldn't judge her.

She nodded.

"I've obviously stayed quiet about it. But when that girl in Kansas went to the police, Osgood sent his goons in to plant evidence, create a false alibi. I *know* what he's capable of. All I want to do is tell the world that it's possible he hurt her. And he tried to shut me up, which pretty shows he did it, huh?"

"Pretty much," Silence said.

In the field, before he pulled a trigger, Silence had to have an overwhelming abundance of evidence. Here in the real world, right was right.

Chelsi smiled at him again, another sad one. "I suppose I'll never see you again."

"Right."

No, she would never see him again. Silence would undoubtedly see her for many years to come—on television, on the magazine racks, maybe even in movies—but to Chelsi, Silence would soon be nothing but a memory.

Chelsi sighed. "Tell Mrs. Enfield I said hello."

"Will do."

Suddenly, Chelsi beamed, that trademark smile of hers finally returning. "You're *not* leaving until I show you something."

She hopped off her sofa and padded across the room in her slippers. When she returned, she had an acoustic guitar. She sat back down, crossed her legs, and readied herself to play.

"I wrote this after seeing how you took care of Mrs. Enfield in Pensacola. I looked at you two and thought, *Beauty and the Beast*. Eventually, the song became just about you. It's called 'The Beast.'" She laughed. "It's sweeter than the title suggests."

She strummed the guitar.

———

A few minutes later, she was done.

And Silence was smiling.

She'd told the truth; it *had* been a sweet song. And as he had when he listened to her songs with Ward in the tailgating area, Silence lost sight of his typical ambivalence toward country music.

"Thank you," he said.

"Of course. That's not going on any album. That was a one-time performance, sir. My goodbye."

# CHAPTER FORTY-SEVEN

*Port-au-Prince, Haiti*

WHERE IN THE world does one hide a world-famous face?

For decades, Octavius Osgood had made a career of doing just the opposite—taking some cute, supple-cheeked visage no one had ever seen and shining a spotlight on it until no one in the world was unfamiliar.

Now he needed to make a world-famous face vanish.

When the world-famous face that needs hiding is black, logic dictates that you hide the face among similar faces. Naturally, Osgood had considered this an opportunity to take a vacation—the Caribbean. But he couldn't go to any of the popular Caribbean destinations. Too risky. Instead of the sandy beaches and bustling street life of Jamaica or Antigua, he opted for a less-traveled destination: Port-au-Prince, Haiti.

As Osgood crossed through the city in the musty rear bench seat of a decades-old taxi, the destitution and poverty overwhelmed him. Everywhere he looked, there were broken-down vehicles, crumbling buildings, and people living on the streets in tattered tents. There was trash strewn everywhere

—plastic bags, rotting food scraps, discarded clothes—all piled up against walls or scattered across sidewalks like debris from a natural disaster. Even more disheartening was how resigned everyone seemed to their fate; there were no protests or angry outbursts here, just silent acceptance that this was all life had to offer.

This wouldn't be the same as Osgood's trip to Saint Martin two years ago...

His entire life was going to be turned upside down, and for now, he couldn't be sure how long. It would be a life of paying in cash, living out of a suitcase, never staying in one place for too long.

After finally exiting the puttering death trap on wheels, he found himself in a tall-ceilinged hotel lobby trying to pass itself off as luxurious. A concoction of smells accosted him— someone's cheap yet overpowering cologne, the damp tang of mold, and a faint trace of lemon cleaner. The walls were adorned with wilting displays of flora in terracotta pots. Osgood's shoes stuck to the layer of grime on the checkered linoleum as he approached the desk, where an attendant in a shirt and tie smiled at him.

Ugh.

This guy was the source of the cheap cologne stench.

"*Hola señor. ¿Cómo estás?*" the man said, hands behind his back and offering a slight bow.

"I don't speak any of that Spanish bullshit, boy!" Osgood said and plopped his bag on the counter. "You got my room ready or not?"

The attendant's smile faltered for a moment before he said, "Yes, *señor* ... er, sir."

He glanced down and flipped through some paperwork. A moment later, he motioned toward the elevator at the end of the lobby.

"Please follow me."

———

Osgood swiped the key from the idiot's hand. "I don't need a tour of this shithole."

The attendant had offered to show Osgood around his room, but after the huff-and-puff treatment, Osgood was in even less of a mood to act like this hotel was anything but a worthless rat's nest.

His room was on the fifth floor, but he and the attendant had gotten off the elevator on the fourth floor. The attendant informed him that the elevator was being serviced. They took the stairs to reach the fifth floor.

When the attendant had explained it all, he'd kept the spurious smile on his lips. Osgood could tell the little shit had been laughing heartily at Osgood on the inside, even more so when Osgood had gotten winded and needed a break at the mid-level landing.

So Osgood sure as hell didn't want a tour of his suite.

He unlocked the door. Stepped inside. Stopped.

Once upon a time, this place must have born a semblance of opulence. Now it was drab and worn-down—tattered upholstery, peeling wallpaper, and a melancholic air that lingered in the stagnant atmosphere.

Osgood sighed.

The suite was on the top floor. Evidently, it had an ocean view. At least there was that. But Osgood couldn't imagine it was a good view, as the hotel was several blocks from the coastline, which meant the "ocean view" would include plenty of dilapidated rooftops.

But no matter what, Osgood had gotten out of the States before shit *completely* hit the fan. Plenty of shit had already been fan-struck.

Egly was dead. Flipped his truck while trying to plow into

tailgaters outside Bear Grove, no doubt his feeble attempt to salvage his failed objective at the arena.

Chelsi had spilled the beans on Osgood. After the concert in Nashville, she'd held an impromptu, live-via-satellite interview with Vanessa Wheatley of *Present Day* explaining Osgood's dealings with young ladies through the years and how that had caused the events with Egly—the murders, the concert tour strife, the disturbance in Jacksonville, and the chaos in Nashville.

Osgood could have fought back—both in the courtroom and, more importantly, in the court of public opinion. But there were some situations that even a formidable man like Osgood recognized to be insurmountable.

He knew when he was beaten.

So he had to flee the U.S.

His future was uncertain only in terms of the details, the specifics, the wheres and the hows. Otherwise, Osgood knew from experience—one of creating wealth out of thin air—that his future was bright.

And it started right here in Haiti.

He dropped his bag on the floor. A small dust cloud lifted. For God's sake, they hadn't even *vacuumed* the place.

He coughed.

Dammit, after he caught his breath and had a chance to wash his face, he would go back down there and—

He screamed.

Someone else was there with him, a burly figure sitting in a nearby chair. The stranger's form was dark and undefined, silhouetted by the drapes that swirled behind him in soft folds.

For a split second, anger rose in Osgood, but it was quickly eclipsed by a primal sort of dread. Innate survival response. Fear.

And a slight sense of recognition...

No, it couldn't be who he thought it was...

He inched closer.

Closer.

The other man didn't budge.

And as he drew within feet of the man, the man's face resolved itself in the shadows.

It *was* the man Osgood had thought it to be.

It was Zack.

The man Chelsi brought onto the security team. Before fleeing Nashville, Osgood had heard that Zack had been in the truck with Egly when it flipped.

Could that mean...

"Uh ... Hello, Zack," Osgood stammered. "Welcome to my new home."

A nervous laugh.

Zack didn't respond.

The man was an intimidating presence, his muscular frame filling the threadbare chair. Dark sunglasses hung from a short-sleeved blue linen shirt worn untucked over khaki pants. His hands rested casually on the ends of the armrests. In one hand was a suppressed pistol.

Osgood gasped.

His attention kept shifting from Zack's cold face to the gun when suddenly he had an idea, a realization.

"Wait..." he said. "A person doesn't party and mingle with as many famous slimeballs as I have without hearing a few rumors. There's this ... legend. About a group of people who hide in plain sight in the American government, people who send out their own illegal assassins to right wrongs." He paused. "You're one of them, aren't you, Zack?"

Zack stared back at him.

"I'm going to die, aren't I?"

Zack nodded.

Osgood shuddered. His eyes flushed warm with tears. And, sure as shit, his lower lip trembled. He bit it.

As soon as this feeling came upon him, though, his momentary lapse into fear changed into a strange sense of melancholic remembrance. He even smiled.

"Chelsi..." he said, looking away from Zack, past the cob-web-riddled ceiling fan to the popcorn texture above. "I know you think I'm a monster and that I probably had nothing but the worst intentions in mind with her, but I wanted more than just a couple of blowjobs."

He scoffed at the ludicrousness of it.

"She's a talent. A natural. The surest star I've ever met, and believe me, I've met plenty. She was born for it. It's right there in her name. *Chelsi Mae Nichols.*" He used an over-the-top Mississippi accent, not his New Orleans drawl, when he said her name. "Have you ever heard a more perfect country music star name in your life?"

He looked at Zack.

No reply. Just those cold eyes.

Reality came back to Osgood then. No more fanciful thoughts of the rawest talent he'd ever discovered, rescuing her from nothingness in Hattiesburg. Time for the devas-tating truth once more.

His own words of a few moments earlier rang through his mind.

*I'm going to die, aren't I?*

"How's this going to happen?" Osgood said.

A moment passed. And when Zack responded, he offered no answer to the query.

"You forced women and teenagers..." he said and swal-lowed. "To perform sex acts."

Osgood couldn't tell if it was a question or a statement. Either way, he knew he should answer truthfully.

"Yes," he said, his voice tiny.

He felt pathetic.

And with that, a surge of energy quickly rushed through him, snapping him into an entirely new state. A few moments ago, he'd been consumed by fear before quickly changing his tune to a sort of defeated nostalgia.

Just as quickly, he pushed that aside for some freakin' swagger!

This situation was winnable.

In the same way that Osgood had rubbed shoulders with many slimeballs over the years, he had also dealt with a lot of do-gooders—maybe not *assassin* do-gooders, but people of the same spirt as Zack. As such, Osgood could get out of this.

Osgood could get out of *anything*. It's what he did, what he'd always done. He was a charmer.

Whether you're dealing with slimeballs or do-gooders or everyday knuckle-dragging buffoons, the only thing you gotta do is level with a person, be genuine with them, reach common ground.

Yes, Osgood could get out of this.

He gave Zack a respectful nod and dropped into the chair across from him, a couple of yards separating them. The chair was wooden with a pair of faded cushions, and its old, dry boards screamed in protest of Osgood's girth. Like Zack, Osgood easily filled the space between the armrests.

"You're right, Zack," Osgood said on a sigh. "Through the years I've had relations with many women and young girls who ended up being clients. But I never *forced* any of them, ya hear? I gave them the opportunity. *An opportunity of a lifetime.* Make me happy, and I'll make you rich and famous. I'm far from the first, and we both know I won't be the last. You've heard of the 'Hollywood casting couch,' haven't you?"

Osgood scoffed, allowing frustration to overtake him for a moment before quickly bringing the smile back to his face and lifting a hand in preemptive defensiveness.

"Now, I know what you're going to say," he continued. "Consensual or not, some of the girls were underage—statutory rape. But hear me out. These girls weren't *that* young, okay? I've been to Thailand, to the Philippines. I've known men who've been with girls..." He trailed off. "Well, you just don't want to know how young we're talking about here, Zack."

Zack said nothing. He didn't move. Not an inch. But Osgood could see the rage surging through the man—the tautness of his neck muscles, the flush on his face, the vein on his temple.

Osgood cleared his throat. "Now, as I understand it, this group of yours—you folks kill murderers, serial rapists, mob bosses. I'm just a pervert who tricked some teenagers into playing with his ding-a-ling."

"You convinced Egly..." Zack said and swallowed. "To kill for you."

Again Osgood cleared his throat. And, again, he knew that being as open and truthful as possible was his best option in this situation.

"Well, yes. But, *but!*, he did the killing. Okay? He did. Not me. I didn't even choose the victims. The guy was a nut, but he was cogent enough to plan out the murders to coincide with her lyrics. The whole *young, old, broken, bold* thing—that was all Egly. It was his idea to frame and slaughter Brom Jenkins, too. I guess the two of them didn't see eye to eye when Egly was a roadie. Other, um, associates of mine supplied him with the security passes, keys, the sniper rifle. So, you see, all I did was plant some ideas in the lunatic's head and offer him a few resources. I'm not a murderer."

Something flashed over Zack's eyes then—a darkness, but also an expression of almost ... *relief!* This theory was confirmed by the slight smirk now playing on the corner of Zack's mouth.

It took Osgood a moment to decipher this reaction. Zack must have accepted what Osgood had just said as a solid confession, justification for what Zack planned on doing. Now the assassin was ready.

*Zack was about to kill him.*

"Probably lots of others..." Zack said, swallowed. "Through the years."

Osgood stared at him. "You mean, did I convince other people to kill for me throughout my career?"

Zack nodded.

Osgood made another quick determination. Zack still meant to kill him, but now he was trying to extract any final intel he could get before the execution.

A flicker of hope danced through Osgood's mind.

Maybe if—

Something warm. On the chair. Shit, he'd pissed himself. Osgood felt it spreading between his smashed-together thighs.

Focus!

What was it again? Yes, honesty! That forthrightness Osgood had been offering might just save his life. Maybe if he came clean entirely, Zack would spare his life. Like in one of those legal TV shows where a character confesses to a crime to avoid the death sentence.

"I ... I ... a few, yes," Osgood said. "But *they* did the killing. Egly and those other fellas. I got in a few tight spots, needed to get myself out of them. Can you blame a guy? Come on. It was never me, though! They killed for me. Egly—"

Zack raised his gun and shot Osgood in the face.

# CHAPTER FORTY-EIGHT

*Lima, Ohio*

LENNY STOOD in the middle of the empty apartment, squinting. Sunlight poured through the tall, arched windows, illuminating every corner, casting bold swashes of brightness and contrasting shadows across the walls. The ceilings were high. The rooms were spacious.

"I was surprised when your friend, Zack, said you only wanted a nine-month lease," said Sarah, the Bay's Edge Luxury Apartments property manager. Her voice echoed harshly on the bare walls, the hardwood floor. "Most people go for at least a year."

Sarah was a petite woman with dark hair pulled back into a tight bun. Her navy blazer and skirt were complemented by a white blouse. She held a clipboard, and, unlike Lenny, she'd been smart enough to remember sunglasses.

Lenny glanced around the bright, cheerful space. Sure, he could afford more than this—a lot more—but still, he felt humbled and unworthy. This wasn't a motel room or a highway rest area somewhere along the Chelsi Nichols tour. This place was ... real.

That's the word his mind kept focusing on—*real*.

The apartment was a *real* place. Lenny was *really* standing in it. And for the next nine months, it was *really* going to be his.

Then he would leave to buy a *real* house.

He could have done all of this on his own. Of course. For many years, Lenny could have done many things differently. But he hadn't. All Lenny had really needed was a helping hand, a little nudge.

Zack had provided that.

The walls were painted a pristine shade of white, and the sun streamed in through the windows, illuminating the rooms, emphasizing the apartment's modern aesthetic and clean lines. It was a reflection of the fresh start Lenny was embarking on.

He grinned, his mind filled with gratitude for Zack's help. He turned to Sarah.

"Yeah, well, I've got big plans," he said. "This will be a temporary home. I'm buying a house soon."

Sarah's smile widened. "That's wonderful! Congrats. In the meantime, I hope you love your time here at Bay's Edge."

"Thanks," Lenny said and reached into his back pocket for his checkbook. "Remind me, how much do I owe you for the first month?"

Sarah grinned almost mischievously. "Zack covered the first month for you."

Lenny shook his head as he returned the checkbook to his pocket.

*Of course he did*, Lenny thought.

Sarah raised the key, jingled it.

Lenny took it.

"Congratulations! Welcome to Bay's Edge," Sarah said.

"We have a great community here. I know you're gonna love it."

She gave him a smile before turning to leave.

The door opened. Then shut.

Then Lenny was alone in the bright, white, empty space

He took a deep breath and explored his new home. Two bedrooms. Two baths. The master bedroom had large windows that framed a view of the park across the street. Lenny imagined waking up to the gentle rays of sunshine and birds chirping—a peaceful start to his days.

The kitchen had sleek countertops, unused appliances, and plenty of storage space. Lenny smelled cleaning materials and brand-new plastics. He envisioned himself preparing delicious meals. And not just for himself. He would host friends and family—the people he'd disappointed. There would be new acquaintances, too. Memories would be made and shared in this apartment.

As Lenny moved from room to room, his thoughts shifted to his loved ones—those friends and family for whom he would soon prepare meals. He imagined their reactions months later when he would share the news of his newly purchased home. They had seen him struggle, witnessed his journey. Now, he could share his successes with them.

But it wasn't just about personal fulfillment. Lenny's heart overflowed with a deep longing to give back to the community that had formed him. Now, with this newfound stability, he could actualize his dreams. He hadn't yet named his future charity, but knew its mission—to provide food, shelter, and medical care for the homeless.

Returning to the master bedroom, he went to the window that overlooked the park. The space outside was lush with trees and shrubs and vibrant green grass. A sparkling pond lay in the center, surrounded by willows that swayed gracefully in the breeze. There was a small playground area and a long winding path, perfect for an afternoon stroll.

Lenny closed his eyes for a moment, savoring the warmth of the sunlight on his face. He knew challenges lay ahead, but he knew he could overcome them. This apartment was more than a temporary base camp; it was a stepping stone toward a brighter future. The world was full of possibilities, and he was ready to seize them.

As he opened his eyes and looked out onto the park once again, he realized his new life had begun.

No better place to start than here.

He turned back around, looked into the empty surroundings.

*Better start by getting some furniture*, he thought.

# CHAPTER FORTY-NINE

*San Mateo, California*

THE BAY AREA offers a lot of coffee shops. Plenty of Internet cafes, too. This was advantageous to Silence.

He sat at a cozy corner table in one of the coffee shops, its walls adorned with vintage posters and local artwork. The aroma of freshly brewed beans filled the air. The place was packed, but the rhythmic hum of conversations was gentle all the same, providing an odd contrast to Silence's dark reasons for being there.

Marlow, his barista, returned. Her vibrant purple hair cascaded down to her shoulders in loose waves. She wore a quirky mix of retro and modern fashion, with piercings on her nostril, tongue, earlobes, and her left cartilage. Her eyes sparkled with vexatious energy as she playfully—but also somewhat legitimately—fussed at Silence.

"It's a shame you're ordering just plain black coffee," she said, pouting her lips mockingly. "We have some kick-ass artisanal blends and flavored concoctions."

"Black," Silence said, standing by the order he'd tried to

give moments earlier upon entering when Marlow had rushed him to a table, saying they were busy, but she'd be with him in just a moment.

Marlow let out a mock sigh.

"Whatever," she said, giving him a quick wink before turning and heading toward the counter.

As she walked away, Silence adjusted his earpiece, ensuring a snug fit. It was linked to a listening device he'd positioned in his parked vehicle just outside. He glanced through the window beside him, past the vehicle, and focused on an Internet cafe across the street.

There he was.

In the cafe.

Slick Chambers.

After all the mental energy Silence had expended on the other side of the country fretfully contemplating the man, there he was. On the other side of the street. A few yards away. Unaware of Silence's presence.

Pointy face. Trim beard. Slicked-back hair. Smug demeanor. He sat on a long wooden bench that faced a line of computers. Though Slick was occupying one of the computer stations, he was turned away from the monitor, engrossed in conversation with a woman whose face remained partially obscured from Silence's view. She wore skin-tight jeans over a skin-tight bodysuit. Late twenties, maybe thirties. Trim physique.

Silence gave his earpiece another adjustment and focused on the conversation. Though the Watchers' tech was top-notch, as always, it wasn't without limitations, and the conversation across the street bore a considerable amount of static.

*No, that's not what I'm asking*, Slick was saying. *Look at me. Do I look the type?*

*Yes, frankly*, the woman said. *What exactly do you think "the type" is?*

When she said this, the woman cocked her head at Slick.

*Listen, I'll pay you for it,* Slick said. *But it's not for me. It's for a ... buddy.*

*You're a hell of a friend.*

Slick snickered. *Not exactly. I run a news tabloid website.* He pointed at the computer behind him. *You know, the Worldwide Web? Wave of the future. You can make money off the Internet! Did you know that? It's wild. Advertisers pay to put ads on websites—just like billboards and magazine ads in the real world. Here's my schtick: I convince people to do illegal things so I can write stories about them. They do the crime, they pay the time, and I cash the check.* Slick laughed. *Never gotten in trouble because I've never done anything illegal.*

*You have now,* the woman said. She hopped off her bench and flashed a badge in Slick's face. *San Mateo Police. You're under arrest for soliciting of prostitution.*

The cafe came alive with people looking in Slick's direction. Some pointed. Some panicked and fled.

And, on his side of the street, Silence grinned.

Specialists had informed Silence that Slick regularly invested Nexus's earnings right back into the website. Apparently, he wasn't a bad businessman. While the money was often put toward the criminal activities Slick exploited, he spent it in ways that left no trail back to himself. He *was* a lawyer, after all.

So to trap him, Silence had to develop a scheme that would both lull Slick into a false sense of security and prove irresistible. To fit those criteria, Silence developed a false narrative that the San Mateo police had a look-the-other-way policy regarding prostitution and that the phenomenon had become well-known online.

How could Slick resist?

Silence watched as the woman slapped cuffs on Slick's wrists. The cafe continued to stare in shock as she hauled him off the bench and marched him away.

Just as the drama unfolded outside, Marlow returned with a steaming mug of black coffee, placing it on the table before Silence.

"Here ya go," she said. "One disgusting cup of old man coffee."

A tray with a tiny porcelain cup was balanced in her left hand. She placed the small cup on the table, a couple of inches from Silence's coffee.

Silence peered inside.

The contents were milky tan. Frothy on top. Steaming.

He looked up at Marlow, blinked.

"Relax, I'm not trying to proselytize you. We're giving them out to everyone."

She pointed to the front counter, where a round table held a collection of the small cups under a handwritten sign that said, *FREE SAMPLES*.

"Just try it," she said.

Silence did so. A tiny sip.

"Well?"

"Not bad."

It really wasn't bad at all.

Marlow gave him another wink. "See?"

She left.

# CHAPTER FIFTY

*Pensacola, Florida*

DARKNESS HAD SETTLED over Pensacola's tranquil East Hill neighborhood. Crickets chirped and neighbors conversed as street lamps cast their glow on the eclectic community. A breeze carried the scents of citronella torches and sizzling grills.

Silence, however, was not savoring the peacefulness as he sat on the chair, looking out from the porch onto the quiet, empty street. Instead, he was tense, prepared.

"Si, please don't do this," Mrs. Enfield said. "You do a lot of good for me, but please don't meddle in my life."

Silence ignored her, still watching the street.

Then he saw the woman he had been waiting for. She was halfway down the block, coming in their direction and carrying a paper bag.

Silence eyed the bag. There was no telling what was in it, but undoubtedly it related to the woman's insidious plan.

He hopped off the chair, headed for the steps.

Mrs. Enfield called out from behind, "Silence, baby, no!"

Silence didn't stop.

Down the steps, down the path, a right turn onto the sidewalk. He stomped forward, and halfway to the corner, he met the woman.

Her eyes widened as she came to a stop. She was pretty, of average height, and with a petite build. Her wavy, brown hair framed her oval face, emphasizing her bright blue eyes. Full lips with red lipstick, her only makeup. She wore a white button-up blouse and faded black Levi's. A pair of leather boots completed the look.

It was her. Miss Maven. Oh, yes. Of that, Silence was one hundred percent certain. Silence had been studying her image all day since he returned to Pensacola, having found it on a flyer in Mrs. Enfield's house. In the flyer image, she'd been wearing some ludicrous robes and beads, nothing like this girl-next-door jeans ensemble she wore now.

But the change of outfit wasn't going to throw Silence. No, he had every detail of that oval-shaped face memorized.

This was her.

This was the scumbag.

"You won't be conning..." Silence said and swallowed. "That old woman." He pointed back to the house. Swallowed. "Leave. Now."

Miss Maven stared at him for a long moment—first with an expression of bewilderment at his terrible voice, then with a look of confusion.

"What?"

"You heard me."

"I ... don't understand."

Just as her clothing made Miss Maven look less like the mythic figure who graced the flyer and more like a genuine person, her voice also had a different quality than what Silence had heard from Mrs. Enfield's answering machine two days earlier. Now, in person, the woman's voice seemed plain, almost vulnerable, not the lofty tones that Silence had heard in the message.

"Mrs. Enfield told me..." Silence said and swallowed. "You're going to connect her..." Another swallow. "To her dead husband." Another swallow. "Leave now, con artist."

Miss Maven's mouth opened. She faltered, then said, "If that's what Rita thought I said, then she misheard. She is in her eighties, you know. I told her I *sensed* Rory from the other side. And I stand by that. But I can't connect the two of them."

Silence scowled at the woman and pointed.

"What's in bag?" He swallowed. "Cash box? Or some bull-shit..." Another swallow. "You're trying to sell her?"

Miss Maven stared at him for another moment. Then she opened the paper bag.

"Banana nut bread. Baked it myself."

Silence looked down. Inside the bag was an aluminum baking tray containing a freshly made loaf of banana nut bread wrapped in cellophane.

Miss Maven closed the bag.

"My name is Lily Morgan. I live here in East Hill, too. Just a few blocks away, off 11th." She pointed behind her. "I am going to charge Rita for this session, yes. Of course. But the bread's on me. Just a nicety, a gesture. I'm not trying to swindle anyone."

Silence could no longer look her in the eye. When he glanced down, he caught a glimpse of the banana nut bread through the gap at the top of the bag.

His nostrils also caught a whiff of it. It smelled fresh. And delicious.

"I take it you're a friend of Rita's?" Lily Morgan said.

Silence looked up, met her gaze again, nodded.

Lily smiled—an understanding, almost sympathetic little twist of the lips.

"Some people see things. They're seers," Lily said. "Surely you must believe that, right? No matter how pragmatic you apparently are."

Several times over the last few days, Silence had been reminded of his innate ability of reading people—first, at the conclusion of the Sioux City mission, then with the Chelsi Nichols happenings.

Though the talent occasionally failed him, he'd always relied on it. When C.C. was alive, she had been proud of this ability of his; she'd encouraged and nurtured it.

C.C., too, had been good at reading people, but she came at it from a much more idiosyncratic angle than Silence. She'd been a quirky individual—despite how rooted in logic her eclecticisms might have been—and, so, she even dipped her toe into the field of psychic matters from time to time.

Unlike Silence, C.C. wouldn't have judged and condemned Miss Maven.

Or, Lily Morgan, rather.

"There are echoes of the dead," Lily continued. "You must believe that, too...?"

Echoes of the dead...

The hairs on Silence's arms stood up.

Silence held full-on conversations in his mind with his deceased fiancée. Suddenly, he felt even worse about assuming Lily Morgan was a con artist.

And, right on cue, the voice of Silence's deceased fiancée spoke to him.

*You've been judgmental again, love,* C.C. said. *Listen to this woman. You could learn a thing or two.*

Lily's expression changed, eyes narrowing as her face tilted slightly. She lifted her free hand.

"May I?"

Silence stared back at her. Blinked. Then nodded.

Lily put her hand on Silence's face. Her palm and fingers

were powder-soft, silky smooth, yet the contact made Silence jump.

Lily's eyes narrowed tighter.

"So much pain," she said. "You've suffered, haven't you?"

Silence didn't respond.

"And you've lost someone. You have a Rory of your own, don't you?"

*C.C. sprawled on the floor.*

*Face mangled.*

*Lying in a puddle of blood.*

Silence was going to leave the question without a response, as he had the previous one, but he sensed his lips moving. The word came out.

"Yes," he said.

Lily stroked his cheek. "I know. Do you want me to—"

"No."

Lily nodded. "Okay."

A few long moments passed as she continued to stare into his eyes, her fingers stroking gently.

"So much pain..."

Finally, she lowered her hand and looked away, peering around him to Mrs. Enfield's house down the block.

"Listen," she said as she returned her attention to him. "After this, I don't think I'm in any position to help your friend tonight. Tell her I'm sorry to delay again, but I'll come back tomorrow. Give her this. Maybe it'll help."

She lifted the bag.

Silence took it, nodded.

One more meaningful glance from Miss Maven, then she turned around and headed down the sidewalk.

Silence, too, retreated. When he stepped back onto the porch, he reached the paper bag toward Mrs. Enfield and said, "She asked me to—"

"I heard every word," Mrs. Enfield said, taking the bag

and placing it beside her on the porch swing's cushion. Her sweet little voice had been a tad less sweet than usual, a bit snippy.

Silence looked over his shoulder, back to the spot on the sidewalk where he'd just confronted Lily Morgan.

The distance was significant, far enough away that the average person wouldn't be able to discern a conversation. But Mrs. Enfield's blindness had enhanced her hearing. The old gal had ears like a bat.

In the same slightly perturbed tone, Mrs. Enfield said, "Sit down, Silence."

Silence obeyed, returning to his chair.

"Do you see what I mean now?" Mrs. Enfield said. "You mustn't immediately judge on first impressions. People might have good intentions, even if it doesn't look like it at the start."

She was right.

Silence didn't respond.

And though C.C. said nothing from the depths of Silence's mind, he could feel her shaking her head at him.

Mrs. Enfield never stayed mad at Silence for long. She smiled, grabbed the paper bag, and extended it in Silence's direction.

"Now, help an old, blind woman," she said. "Go to the kitchen and slice this banana bread up so we can get to eatin'. And don't forget the butter."

Silence stood up and took the bag.

"Yes, ma'am," he said.

# ALSO BY ERIK CARTER

*The Skinny*

*No Fake*

Novella

*Get Down*

# ACKNOWLEDGMENTS

For their involvement with *A Strangled Cry*, I would like to give a sincere thank you to:

My ARC readers, for providing reviews and catching typos. Thanks!

Made in United States
North Haven, CT
28 August 2023

40870229R00134